KISS OF THE SWAN

NATALINA REIS

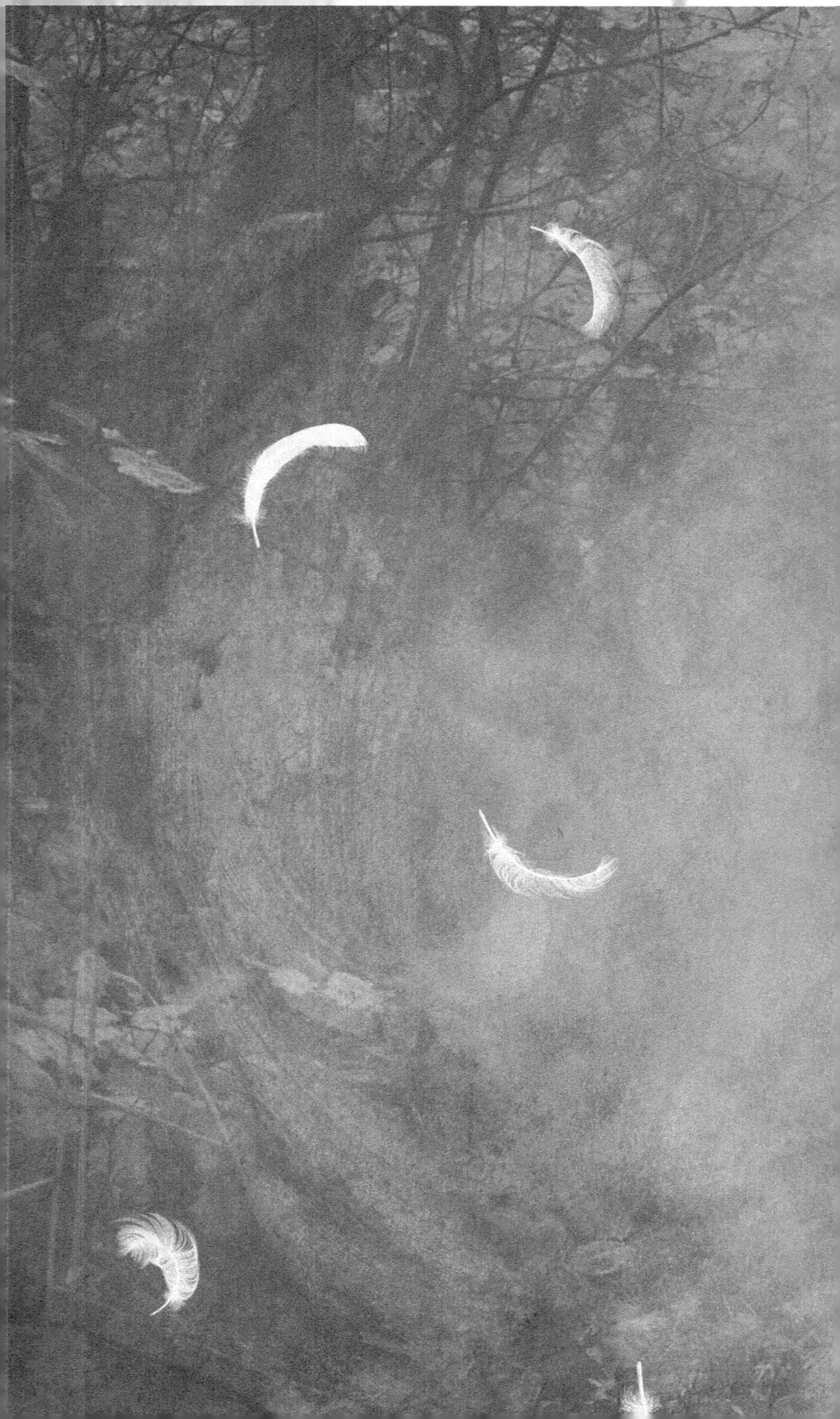

Kiss of the Swan

Natalina Reis

Kiss of the Swan

Cover design: Adrijana Cernic
Interior design: RMGraphX

ISBN: 978-1-7374413-1-1

DEDICATION

This book is for my grandma, Alice, who introduced me to the Brothers Grimm's Fairytales in her kitchen while I sat at the large, marble-top table watching her cook. Obrigado, avó.

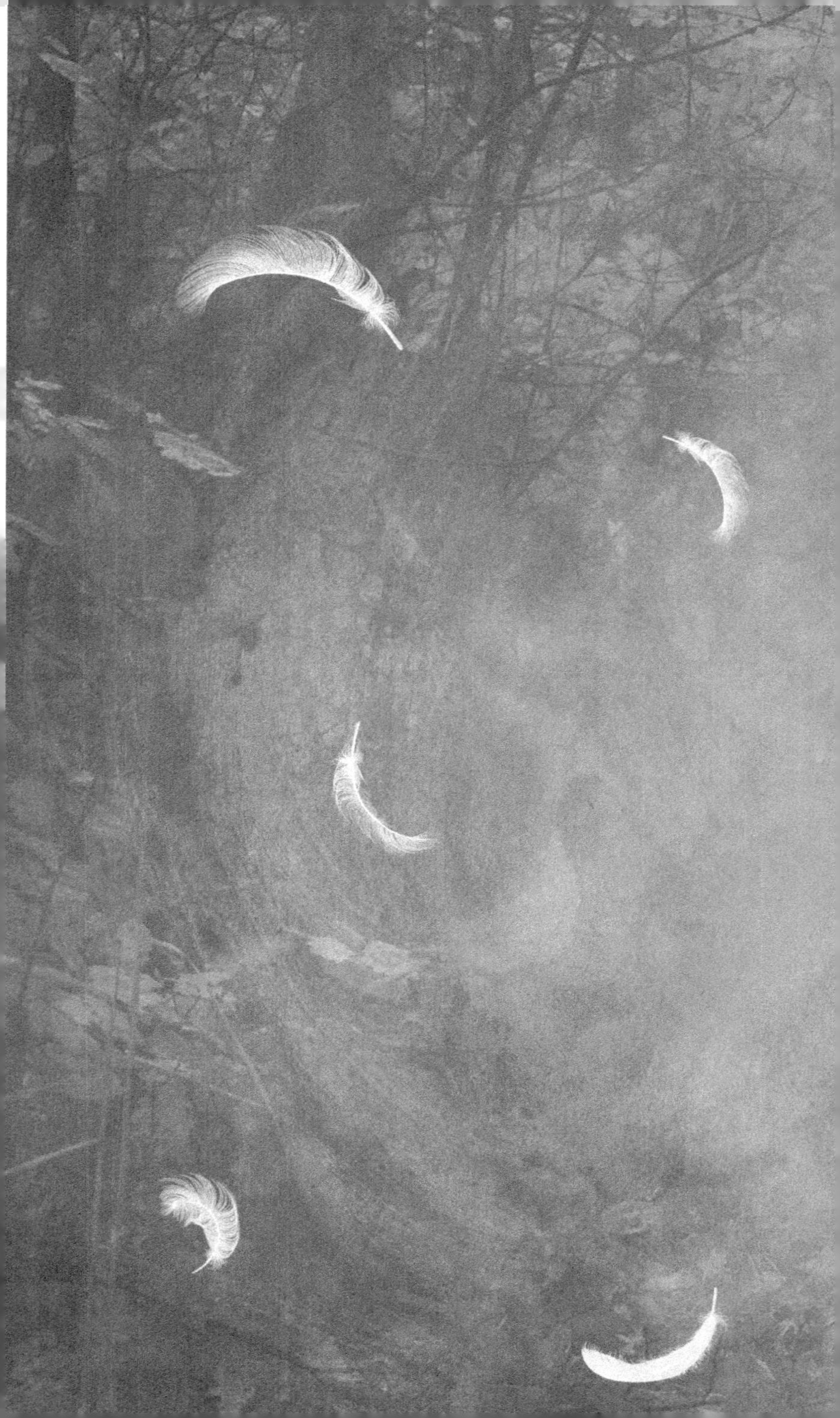

CHAPTER ONE
Prologue

The baby's wail was heard across the land, and everyone knew this was not to be a normal child.

The King and Queen of Nem had been childless for many years. A battalion of women was enlisted for the king to impregnate, but no baby was ever begotten. This was, of course, not public knowledge, for the king prided himself of his male prowess, and to admit to his court and subjects that his seed was not strong enough to bear fruit would have been an embarrassment. So, he continued to bed every eligible female in town, beheading them afterward when they didn't yield a pregnancy.

One day, a woman who claimed to be a powerful witch stormed into the palace, demanding an audience with the king. This was unheard of since all the witches had been exterminated years ago.

"Tell her to leave," King Rian had said, his face

still buried between the breasts of his latest concubine. "I'm busy."

The little eunuch who served the king with the utmost discretion delivered the royal message and came back with another one. "She says she won't leave, Your Majesty," the man said, his gaze on the floor. "She told me to let you know she can guarantee you a royal heir."

That caught the king's attention. "Who is she?" he asked, dropping his lover on the pillow and swinging his legs over the edge of the bed to move into a sitting position.

The eunuch peeked at the almost unconscious concubine, lying naked on the white linen, and wondered what kind of drug the monarch had used on her this time. "Her name is Dochrach, and she says she has powerful magic."

Naked as the day he was born, the king stood up. "Bring me those robes," he ordered, pointing at some discarded clothes on a chair. "I will grant her a conference. If she is lying, I will chop her to pieces."

Dochrach was indeed a witch who, after bedding the wicked king, quickly became pregnant, much to the monarch's delight. The crown was finally going to have an heir. Unexpectedly, the witch forbade any visits from the royals throughout her pregnancy, a fact that didn't bother the king in the least—less to worry about. When it was time to give birth, she merely called a midwife and delivered the infant in the privacy of her quarters. Soon afterward, Dochrach had the baby delivered directly to his father by a wet nurse with instructions that the witch must be invited to the boy's naming ceremony and given the highest noble title in the land.

King Rian had no intentions of doing what she requested.

"Tell the guards to capture Dochrach when she comes to the festivities," he told the eunuch. He would swiftly behead her like he had all the other women and never have to spare her another thought.

On the day of the naming, everyone who was anyone was invited, except for Dochrach. Soldiers flooded the streets and every inch of the palace, looking out for the witch, but she couldn't be found.

In a room packed with noblemen and foreign dignitaries, King Rian haughtily raised his child above his head and presented the infant boy to the court.

"This is my royal heir, Prince Ríoga, who will take my throne someday," he announced to the crowd.

A murmur of voices ran through the crowd like a wave. Many had thought this day would never come. Men and women alike gaped in wonder and relief at their king; there wasn't a single family in the kingdom who didn't fear their daughters would have been taken to the palace to never return. Now that the monarch had an heir, maybe they could finally sleep in peace.

The baby had just been returned to his cot when a wild wind blew the doors open, and every hat, every headdress in the room flew up in the air. Before the king had the time to call the soldiers, the doors slammed shut, and Dochrach materialized in the center of the room, magnificent in a dress that seemed as if made of a star-studded midnight sky.

"How dare you come in uninvited?" Despite the arrogance in his voice, the king had paled at the sight of his child's mother.

The witch laughed and stepped closer to the baby's crib. "I came to offer my gift, Your Majesty," she said with a slight bow of the head. "After all, there is a special place in my heart for this child."

The eunuch snorted into his sleeve, and the king threw him a look that could melt diamonds. "Stop her, you fool," he hissed between his teeth. The eunuch shrugged. How could such a little man like him stop a mighty witch?

Dochrach reached the side of the bassinet and leaned over the baby with a predatory smile. "How adorable Mí-ádh is," she said with a coo.

"His name is Ríoga," the monarch protested in a shaky voice, not daring to take a step forward.

She laughed again. "No, it is not." The witch punctuated her words with a dismissive gesture of her hand. "This baby is cursed, so his name will be Mí-ádh."

The eunuch watched as King Rian swallowed, his Adam's apple bobbing up and down in his mighty neck. "What do you mean he's cursed?"

"Well, technically, he's not. Yet!" Dochrach circled the crib like a vulture over carrion. "But he will be when the time comes." Her soft, almost tender tone was more frightening than anything else. From the doors, a racket arose, soldiers trying to get inside. She cackled this time, throwing her head back. "Oh dear, I must have sealed the doors. Well, they can come in after I'm finished."

The king took a few steps backward. "What are you going to do? Kill my son?"

The woman clicked her tongue and shook her head. "Of course not. Why would I do such a thing? No, I want you to watch him grow into a toddler and then a boy and a man. I want you to love him and dream of what he will one day be, your one and only child." The eunuch scratched his nose. The conversation was not going where he'd thought it would. "Then, when you love him fiercely…" She closed her fist in the air as if catching a fly. "Then, I will take him away from you. But don't worry, I won't kill him."

All color had gone from the king's already pale face, but he didn't have enough courage to try and stop the witch. He looked at the eunuch again as if he could do anything.

"I'm sorry I didn't invite you, my dear Dochrach," Rian said, his lips shaking. "That's because I was going to invite you for a much bigger celebration later this week."

Dochrach tilted her head to the side. "Aww, that's

sweet of you," she cooed, a saccharine smile on her lips. "Unfortunately, it's too late now. Your sweet boy—well, not so sweet as you'll find out soon enough—will come to me when he turns eighteen, and I will grant him eternal sleep. And because I hate to think of my child alone in the world of dreams and nightmares, I will send the whole court—you included, Your Majesty—with him."

Unwisely, the king laughed. "You're crazy. Why would my son seek you out?"

"Because, Your Majesty, I know where he lives, and I made him who he will be. He will come to see me when it's time." She wiggled her fingers a couple times and vanished.

It was then that the child, who had been quiet all along, let out the most awful, blood-curdling wail the kingdom had ever heard. The curse had been cast.

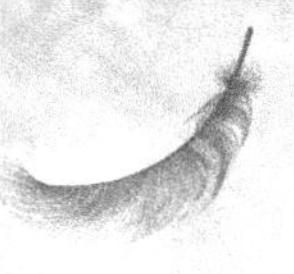

CHAPTER TWO
In the Beginning

Despite the heat, Cathal shivered. Where could that brat be? The last time Odhran had escaped Cathal's watchful eye, he had to rescue his brother from the clutches of a bear—a cub, really, but momma bear couldn't have been too far.

"Odhran, where in heaven's name are you?" he yelled out, spinning around and scanning the land.

There weren't that many places for his seven-year-old brother to hide. The valley where they lived was as scarcely forested as it was populated. No matter in what direction his gaze roamed, fields of knee-high grasses swayed in the soft breeze. When he was his brother's age, he had often thought that graceful and sensual sway looked an awful lot like their mother's hair blowing in the wind. That was eleven years ago, though; their beautiful, free-spirited mother had been out of their lives for at least half as long.

Where was that brat? Was he in danger again? "Odhran! Answer me, you puny elf." Anger mixed with worry tightened his chest. Odhran had taken one of his brother's bows with him. Cathal had to find him before he did something stupid. "You'll go without supper if you don't answer me."

The cove was just ahead, half protected by sand dunes and the only high vegetation in the area. Maybe the boy had gone fishing. But he had taken the bow, not the fishing pole. And then, there was the story Tadhg had unwisely spun by the fire last night. Stupid of him to tell the child about the swans. Tadhg was a year older than Cathal, an adult. Why offer such a story to a boy who he knew to be such a wild cannon? Odhran had never been like the other children; something in his brain made him reckless and even cruel sometimes.

A loud honk made him whip his head toward the beach. "Oh shit, no. The swans." Cathal took off running, his heart jumping to his throat, a silent prayer on his tongue, "Please, Guardians, don't let him hurt the swans."

He cleared around the dunes that obscured the sandy beach and blanched. His brother was standing a few feet away, bowstring drawn as far as his little arms would allow and pointed at a wedge of swans flying low over the water. "Stop, Odhram!" Cathal yelled, resuming his running toward the boy. "Stop."

The boy pointed a little higher, and with a chuckle, he released the string. The arrow flew in an upward curve and hit one of the large birds. The graceful creature let out a sound that eerily resembled a scream and began to plummet toward the ocean waters as the others dispersed in a panic of honks and wings.

"I got one, Cathal, I got one," the boy yelled, dropping the bow in the sand and clapping. "We can eat it for dinner tomorrow."

Blood had left Cathal's face. His brother had shot one of the royal swans. If anyone found out, the whole family would be executed on the spot. "You wicked boy, you know better. Do you want to go to prison?"

Odhran glanced at him, a frown on his face. "What do you mean? They were out of the island and in our lands."

Cathal shook his head. "Stupid kid, we have no lands," he said, watching as the animal plunged into the ocean with a big splash. "We live on borrowed land, fool. I told you last night those swans are sacred. No one is allowed to touch them."

The boy smirked. "Then we need to eat it quickly so no one will find out."

At the end of his rope, Cathal raised his hand to hit his younger brother. The boy didn't even cringe. The older Odhran got, the less he feared his elders. Cathal lowered his hand and said, "Go home, now. I will take care of the swan."

The youngster groaned, "And take all the credit for catching dinner? No way. I'm staying."

Cathal looked around him and pulled a long switch

from the soil, and advanced toward the boy. "Go now, or I will whip your butt," he threatened. "You got us in enough trouble already. What makes you think I want to take credit for killing one of the king's swans?" He raised the switch above his head and took another step forward. "Go now!"

This time, the threat hit its mark, and the boy ran away, shouting back curses. Cathal surveyed the waters, searching for the fallen swan, and quickly spotted a white shape floating a few feet in. He discarded his shoes by the bow, took off his shirt, and waded in until he reached the dead animal. Fighting the pull of the tide, Cathal slipped his arms beneath the bird and dragged it close to him. He would bury the swan somewhere no one could find it. Everyone knew—including his little brother—that the swans were untouchable, protected by the king, and kept on an island off the coast. Odhram didn't care; after all, he didn't care about much other than eating and having fun. Sometimes, Cathal wondered whether their mother's death had something to do with the boy's lack of empathy and kindness.

The swan, white feathers stained with blood, hung limply from Cathal's arms. Its heavy weight made his walk—first in the water and then on the sand—difficult and slow. There was an area covered in grasses and other vegetation between two dunes that looked like a good place to hide the animal, so he made his way there. Gently, he set the bird down on the grassy sand

and began digging a hole beside it. A scoop of any kind would have made his work easier, but as it was, he only had his hands to dig in the slippery sand.

A rustling sound startled him. Freezing as to not give his location away, Cathal scanned the area but couldn't see anything. Then he heard it again, and it seemed as if it was coming from nearby. A slight movement caught his eye. Was the swan still alive? He peered closer, and much to his surprise, the bird's chest rose with a shallow breath.

It's alive!

Cathal was not sure if that was good or if it complicated things; after all, if the bird was dead, he could at least hide the body and hope no one would ever find it. But if the swan was still alive, what was he supposed to do? Kill it?

He shook his head, crouching next to the bird. "No, no, I will have to heal it back to health," he murmured to himself. "It's the right thing to do." Even if he was running the risk of being discovered and sentenced to death along with his whole family.

Hesitantly at first, Cathal kneeled closer to the animal and gently examined the wound. The arrow had gone completely through the bird's wing but didn't seem to have damaged anything vital. He smacked his forehead, mad at himself that he hadn't thought to check first. A few more minutes, and he would have buried a live creature.

Sitting back on his heels, he thought for a moment.

"Where can I take the swan and hide it?" Thankfully, there weren't many people around. His small house sheltered himself, his brother, and Mhamó, his maternal grandmother. The next house was at least two miles off, and the valley offered so little in terms of natural resources, it was rare for anyone to venture their way. "The *scioból*!" The old, abandoned barn was rumored to be haunted, and even Odhran didn't dare enter it for fear of the ghosts.

Decision made, Cathal slipped his arms under the bird and lifted it. He sighed deeply and began the long walk to the *scioból*, hoping no one would spot him on the way there. The swan was unexpectedly warm against his chest, the beating of its heart keeping pace with his own. Cathal relaxed his hold a bit as his heart filled with a strange sense of familiarity, of kinship as if he was now somehow connected to the animal.

"No, no," he muttered, picking up the pace. "Stop being ridiculous. This is just a bird. There's no connection." Yet, as he continued his walk across the valley, his heart sang a different tune.

SNEAKING food out was turning out to be a lot harder than Cathal thought. Odhran had been suspicious and sullen since the incident with the swan earlier that week, and his gaze seemed to follow Cathal's every move. So, he waited until his brother left with Mhamó to feed the chickens to slip a slice of bread and some discarded lettuce and spinach into a small pouch hidden under his shirt. He would go see the swan in a couple hours as soon as his family was asleep.

"You look pale," Mhamó had said that morning. It was no wonder; he had been staying up late every night, nursing the swan back to health. Daily life didn't stop with all its responsibilities and chores, so he stumbled through each day, wanting to do nothing more than collapse on his bed for a nap.

"You're up to something," his brother said with a sideways glance. Cathal couldn't make him suspicious, or he was sure to attract Odhran's curiosity. The last thing he wanted was for his brother to find out he was harboring and taking care of one of the sacred royal swans. "What are you hiding?"

"Don't be stupid," Cathal replied with an emphatic shake of the head. "What can I possibly be hiding?"

Odhran smirked. "Do you have a secret girlfriend?" Cathal hoped his relief was not too obvious, but he was glad his brother thought he was having some love affair. Anything was better than the truth. "Are you seeing a married woman?"

Mhamó clicked her tongue. "Stop talking nonsense, boy. Your brother is too young and too honorable to do such a thing. Eat your supper."

The boy grumbled but obeyed, returning his full attention to the meager meal in front of him. Cathal hadn't been able to earn a lot of coin to buy food in town for the past week. Tired as he was, no one was willing to hire him. He didn't have a steady job; instead, he took whatever work the villagers would throw his way: cleaning dung, helping in the fields, plucking chickens, or—if he was lucky—doing odd jobs for the noble families in town.

His mother had told him often that his father was a nobleman who had tragically died before marrying her, but Cathal had no illusions; there was such an age difference between him and his brother that the chances of them sharing the same father were extremely slim. Their mother had been a beautiful woman with long, thick autumn hair who caught every male's eye whenever she went by. She was also poor and lonely, and he was certain it wouldn't have been hard for a honeyed-tongue male to sway her into his bed.

He had almost nodded off as he sat, pretending to be reading and waiting for both his brother and grandmother, who slept in the loft over his bed, to fall asleep. Odhran was a heavy sleeper who not even an earthquake could stir awake, and Mhamó was old and hard of hearing, so as soon as he heard his brother's soft snores, Cathal was off to the *scioból*.

The night was chilly despite the summer heat that turned everything brown during the day, and for a moment, he considered going back to fetch a sweater but decided against it. It wasn't worth the risk, and the *scioból* was normally warm after absorbing the sun's rays all day. The small structure was at the edge of what his brother called their land—the barren spread that they rented from a local lord in return for its keep. What made it inhospitable also made it easy to take care of; there was no vegetation to tend other than the wild grasses that required zero care and no farming land except the modest rectangle of beaten dirt by the house where they grew a few vegetables. A large chicken coop, the only thing that seemed to thrive in that place, stood not too far from their house. Mhamó insisted on taking care of the borrowed chickens with the help of Odhran, who didn't mind as long as he could chase the poor fowl around the coop. Every week, Cathal took how many chickens the landlord had asked for, plus most of the eggs, to the manor in town.

At the sight of the decrepit building, Cathal let out a sigh of relief. He was bone tired and shivering and couldn't wait to bask in its warmth inside. He moved the unhinged door, a simple slat of moldy wood, to the side and walked in, making sure to cover the doorway behind him. The moonlight coming through the small windows was enough to prevent him from tripping over the few pieces of broken furniture still lingering around. Gingerly, he stepped around the three-legged table he had propped against a wall and crouched by the pile of dried grasses where he had settled the wounded swan.

Afraid that someone would see the light, he only allowed himself the soft glow of a jar packed with fireflies. He set it down on the dirt floor and touched the swan lightly.

"It's me, Cathal." The same words he said every night.

The swan moved, its large orange and black beak emerging from between its folded wings. It made a tiny sound that Cathal couldn't put a name to and then bumped its graceful head into his chest in greeting. The first couple of times Cathal had come to take care of it, the bird had been panicky and suspicious and tried to attack him. The loss of blood had weakened it, so it was no threat for Cathal, but it made it hard to treat its wound. After a while, the swan seemed to realize Cathal was there to help it and started to welcome his visits and his attention.

Cathal unfolded the injured wing. "Let's have a look." Some of the white feathers were still stained with blood, but he had managed to wipe most of it off. On the base of its neck, where it connected with the wing, there was an odd black marking that resembled a constellation of stars, Virgo maybe. Cathal had never seen a swan with those markings, but then again, no one dared to come that close to the sacred birds. "The wound has healed nicely," he said, examining the area with his fingers. "You should be able to fly now and join your family."

Strangely, the animal seemed to understand his

words and stretched its long neck to stare at him. He would miss the bird, his only company for the past couple of weeks—since his mother had died if he was honest with himself. But this was a forbidden animal, protected by the crown and rumored to have a special kind of magic. He had to let it go, and the sooner, the better.

The swan nuzzled him, and he chuckled. "I'll miss you too," he whispered. His eyes were growing heavy, and before he knew it, he had stretched beside the animal on the bed of grasses and drifted off to sleep. He was only half-aware that the swan had draped its wing over his chest and nestled its head on his shoulder.

CHAPTER THREE

The Island

Cathal

"I'm going to kill you, you little weasel," Cathal mumbled under his breath while he crouched behind a bright green bush, the likes of which he had never seen. "I'm going to roast you for dinner and enjoy every bite."

Of course, he would never hurt his brother, but he would certainly give him a good spanking this time. The older Odhran got, the more unruly and wicked he became, and Cathal couldn't keep count of the times he had to bail his brother out of trouble. His back still smarted from a whipping he had taken instead of Odhran a mere week ago when Odhran had stolen two sweet buns from a market vendor in town. Now, here he was again, putting himself in danger for the sake of his wayward sibling. Were Cathal caught this time, a beating would be the least of his worries. Trespassing on Swan Island was a major crime that warranted immediate execution, but it was his duty to protect his witless brother.

He should have known something was wrong when Cathal woke up to a quiet house. Seventeen-year-old Odhran was not known for being still; his body was in constant movement, and his brain never stopped concocting trouble. Cathal woke up every morning to the sound of his grandma yelling threats at Odhran for something he had done: eaten all the food Mhamó had cooked for breakfast or plucked feathers off her prize chicken. He was always up to no good, and no number of beatings or lectures changed his wicked ways. That morning, all was quiet, and Cathal allowed himself a moment of peace before realizing the silence boded nothing except trouble.

"Where's Odhran, Mhamó?" he had asked his grandma as soon as he reached her in the chicken coop. His brother was nowhere to be seen.

The old woman turned her time-worn face to him and hesitated. "Isn't he with you?" He shook his head, the heaviness of worry beginning to weigh him down. "He said he was going hunting with you."

Cathal only went hunting for predators, the wolves that ventured into that barren land to steal their chickens once in a while, or the snakes and rats that sneaked up at night to steal their eggs. But he never hunted for food, so what was his brother going on about?

"He took the bow and said he was meeting you at the island."

What island? The only island he knew about was Swan Island, and even his brother wouldn't be crazy as to go there. Or would he? "Did he take Asal?" The old donkey was left alone most of the time, its stubbornness growing exponentially with the years, but his brother took pleasure in tiring the old mount by riding him constantly, even small distances.

"No, he said he didn't need the donkey," Mhamó said, scratching her snow-white head. "He said he would take the boat instead. I should have known he was up to something, that little *teallaire*."

Why would he take the dinghy to go hunting? A terrible thought crossed his mind. "Mhamó, what day is today?"

The old woman scratched her head again, deep in thought, before answering, "September twenty-four."

Cathal's stomach twisted. "The equinox." One of the only four times of the year when it was possible for mere mortals like them to cross over to Swan Island. His brother had been boasting about crossing it for years, claiming he would hunt the swans and bring back their gizzards. He even bet money he didn't have with some of the local men. Cathal had always dismissed it as pure bravado, a need to show off to the other males in town and maybe attract some of the females, but now, he chided himself for being a fool. The sacred swans' gizzards were fabled to have magic and be the cure for all kinds of illnesses. Odhran would not let an opportunity to make a fortune pass by, even if it meant doing something dangerous and illegal.

The crossover was so easy that he wondered for a brief moment why more people hadn't tried to do it, but then he remembered the consequences for such an act; those who had indeed tried were most likely underground feeding maggots. His brother had taken their dinghy, so he had to improvise with the old door from the *scioból* as a raft of sorts. Cathal said a short prayer, hoping it would hold until he reached the gate, got on it, and used another slat of wood to paddle his way across the cove.

Legend said the gate to Swan Island was invisible but somewhere not far from the shore; thus, he trained his keen eyes on the horizon where the calm waters of the inlet met its wilder ocean side. He was not sure what he was looking for—a sign of some kind, a hint— but he found it, a slight shimmering of the air almost exactly in the center of the small mouth of the cove. He doubled his efforts to reach it, the makeshift raft barely floating as he plunged and dragged the slip of wood in the water, bringing himself slowly closer and closer to the gate. It occurred to him as he was crossing it that this might be the last time he saw the cove, that he might never return.

Hidden behind the bush, he scanned the area but couldn't locate Odhran anywhere. The foolish teenager had a few hours on him. The Guardians only knew where he might be. Dead? Quite possibly, but Cathal hoped not; as much of a pain as his younger brother was, Odhran was his blood, and he had promised his mother to watch and protect him. Only that promise kept him from running back to that gate to hide in the safety of the cove.

Swan Island was not what he expected, even though he couldn't have quite explained what that was. In stark contrast with where he made his home, the island was a luxuriant festival for the senses, covered in greenery and flowers, ponds and creeks that burbled as they flowed over rocks, and the heady scent of flowers and herbs—lavender and mint—mixed with the sweet tang of citrus. So rich that Cathal found it hard to concentrate on the reason he was there, overwhelmed by his own five senses.

He shook his head, fighting against the urge to take a long sniff of air. "Focus, Cathal," he told himself, pinching the underside of his arm until it hurt. He needed something to keep him grounded. "You need to find your brother."

Nothing living seemed to be abroad; therefore, he risked rising from his hideout and heading down the grassy path. Despite the wildness of the surroundings, the grass was manicured and seemed to demand it be followed. Cathal suspected it was a trap, but he didn't have a lot of choices left. Gingerly, and with an abundance of caution, he made his way down the path and between the tall trees that edged it. There were trees of every kind, some he didn't even recognize but suspected shouldn't be growing alongside the others: cold-weather trees mixed and mingled with those of warmer climates in an unnatural harmony. But then again, what had he expected from an island suspended in the air like a solid cloud? Magic was at work here; there was no denying it.

The path suddenly veered to the right and erupted from in between two giant sequoias into what resembled a garden—not as structured as the ones he had seen at the manors in town, but tamer than the rest of the island. A lake stretched out between grass-covered banks shaded by willows, red maples, dogwoods, and peach trees. Cathal's mouth dropped open. He had never seen such beauty, and, for a moment, he was paralyzed by it.

A loud honk like that of a trumpet exploded behind him, but he had no time to turn around; something swiped against his legs, making him lose his balance and fall face-first into the grass. Managing to roll over, Cathal was faced with a group of hissing swans, their long necks curved backward, and their powerful wings spread wide. He tried to scuttle back on his hands, but one of the swans lunged forward and punched him in the chest with its hard beak, knocking the air out of him. Choking, Cathal brought his arms up to protect himself, but the birds charged forward and attacked him with their bills and wings.

"I mean you no harm," he yelled out as soon as he

could inhale air. "Please, listen to me."

When he thought he was done for, seriously bruised and bleeding, the swans suddenly stopped as a young woman with long dark hair and dressed in a flowing white dress appeared out of nowhere. "Let's take him to the Queen," she said.

Cathal knew he must have been hallucinating, but he could have sworn the swans changed into human forms—men and women in ethereal white robes—right before total darkness descended upon him.

SOMETHING smelled wonderful. His mind was muddled, and he couldn't open his eyes, but Cathal delighted on the scent that tickled his nose: a mixture of lavender and lemon. He licked his dry lips and wished he hadn't; they tasted of rotten blood and felt like sandpaper. *I need water.* But could he even talk? He seemed to have lost control of his own body as if his brain had disconnected from the rest of him.

As if guessing his thoughts, someone slipped an arm behind his head and propped him up slightly before spooning delicious cool water between his lips. In his greed, he choked a few times, but the water tasted like the best nectar the world had to offer. When his head was gently set down on the pillow, he whispered a thank you, not sure anyone could hear it.

"Sleep now," a lovely female voice said. "I put a sedative in your water to help you recover. I will come back in a few hours."

Cathal struggled to open his eyes but wasn't able to do more than merely lift his eyelids enough to see the contours of a human form walking away from him. Whatever sedative she had given him took effect almost immediately, and he wandered off to sleep.

"How do you feel?" The soothing female voice wrenched him from a dreamless slumber. He tried to open his eyes and was surprised when he could. Cathal blinked a few times, adjusting to the brightness, and then found the woman sitting on the edge of the bed. "I have some food on its way, but would you like more water?"

He opened his mouth but said nothing, stunned by the beauty of the female beside him. She was small, smaller even than his five-foot-four grandmother, and thin; the bones on her pretty face so fine, it looked as if she could easily break. Her hair was a fiery halo of curls that fell onto her shoulders, highlighting her ivory skin. Her blue-green eyes were the stars in a sky of golden freckles, crowned by perfectly arched eyebrows.

A kind smile stretched on her lips. "Well? Do you want some water?" He belatedly nodded, heat rising up his neck and into his face. He'd been shamelessly staring at her. If she minded, she didn't show it. She grabbed the bowl from a side table and began again spooning water into his mouth. "You need to take it easy for a few days," she said, her voice as melodic as a song. "My brothers and sisters were a bit too rough on you, thinking you were dangerous like the boy who came before you. I apologize for them."

Cathal suddenly remembered what he was doing on the island. "My brother, is he all right?" Realizing she didn't know who they were, he added, "He came before me, teenager, shorter than me with blond hair and a crescent-shaped scar on his neck."

Her smile died as she lowered the spoon into the bowl. "He's your brother?"

He nodded. "Yes, Odhran. He came here without authorization. I chased him down to bring him back home." The angry look on her face didn't bode well. "Have you seen him?"

"He shot a few of my siblings," she said, ice in her voice. "He's been taken to jail and will be sentenced soon."

Cathal's heart skipped a beat, and a cold shiver ran through him. Damned brat had hurt people on the island. What was wrong with him? He had tried to bring up Odhran to be a decent man but failed miserably.

"Did he also hurt any of the sacred swans?" he asked, afraid of what the answer might be. "He didn't kill anyone, did he?"

The red-haired woman lowered her eyes to her lap, where she was still holding the bowl of water. "No one was killed, but yes, he has hurt some of the swans."

A stab of shame and horror made him wince. "Oh, my Guardians. I'm so sorry. He's young and stupid." The same old excuses for his brother's cruel behavior. When would he stop covering up for Odhran? "I brought him up wrong. It's my fault." He knew plenty well it wasn't; the young man had always been taught to do the right thing by his mother and then by Cathal and his grandmother. There was something wrong with the boy's heart and soul as if he did not have one or the other.

The flutter of the woman's green eyes made him tingle all over. "Not your fault, Cathal," she said in a feathery voice. "There is evil inside him."

How did she know his name? Had he told her in his sleep? Had his brother mentioned it to her or the others?

"Who are you?" he asked, curiosity winning over caution. Such a beautiful creature living on Swan Island, he had to wonder what her purpose was. Did the humans living there serve the king? Were they the sacred birds' keepers?

"My name is Eala," she whispered, setting the bowl down on the table. She opened her mouth to say something else, but another woman, taller and older, walked into the room with a tray in her hands. "Here's your food." She waved the other closer. "Bring it to his bed, Laoise."

The other woman obediently brought the tray to

set it down on top of the bed, then bowed to Eala. "Anything else, my Queen?"

Queen? This ethereal creature was a queen? Why had he never heard any stories about royalty on the sky island?

Eala shook her head. "No, thank you. You may leave."

Laoise hesitated for a second. "But, my Queen, what shall we do about the other—"

The queen stopped her with a raised hand. "We'll talk about it later," she said, an edge to her tone. "Right now, our guest needs to recover from the injuries our brothers and sisters caused." The other woman opened her mouth as if to say something, but Eala cut her off. "We *will* talk about it later." There was a finality, a sense of authority in her words. Laoise didn't argue, taking a quick bow before leaving the room.

"Was she talking about my brother?" Cathal asked, worry fighting with anger, two of the usual feelings his brother always stirred in him. "What are you going to do with him?"

She licked her full bow-shaped lips. "We can discuss that after you are well." She had referred to him as a guest. Did that mean he wasn't in any danger for trespassing on the island? "Eat." She pointed at the tray where two plates displayed a colorful and delicious-looking array of food. There were fruits he had only seen in books and vegetables whose names he couldn't even guess. *No meat.* Even the porridge was sprinkled with petals of a purple flower he didn't recognize.

Cathal wanted to know what was going to happen to his brother, but he was ravenous. It occurred to him that he had no idea how long he had been sleeping. The gate would close in a few days, and if they couldn't leave before then, they would be trapped on that island until the winter solstice. What would happen to their Mhamó with no one to take the chickens and eggs to the landlord?

"The gate will close, and my grandmother—" Eala covered his hand with hers in a comforting gesture that instead had his heart galloping like a wild horse. "She's old," he added weakly.

"Everything will be taken care of," she assured him, squeezing his hand. "Eat and rest. Let me take care of everything else. Your grandmother will be fine."

He had no reason to believe her, but he did anyway. There was something in her voice, something in the way she looked at him that was both familiar and reassuring. He knew that, for whatever reason, she had no intention of hurting him. Despite his trespassing, his brother's wicked ways, and the wounded swans, she wished him no harm. So, after a brief moment of hesitation, he did as she told him; he ate while she watched him in silence and then slid down under the sheets and fell asleep again.

CHAPTER FOUR

Eala

Eala

The white feather hovered in the air for a few seconds before drifting slowly to the ground. Eala followed its progress with her eyes, her mind elsewhere. Laoise, who was standing a few feet away, threw her a worried glance, and Eala offered her a half-hearted smile.

"What's wrong, Laoise?" she asked, knowing full well what concerned the other woman.

"You're not yourself lately, my Queen," her attendant said, lowering her eyes to the ground. "I worry that this man we caught trespassing will be your undoing."

Eala sighed and plucked another feather from her dress. "You mean you worry it will be all of *your* undoings?" She knew her siblings truly loved and cherished her, but as the queen, bitterness sometimes burned in her tongue. Whatever happened to her happened to all her eleven siblings. There was no room for selfishness in her life; whatever she did, whatever she decided, had to be with all of them in mind. Always. "Sorry, I'm being unfair." She blew the feather away and stood up to face her older sister. "You know I would never do anything to hurt you, right? You're my brothers and sisters, and I will always put you before me."

Laoise raised her eyes. "I know, my Queen."

"Stop calling me that." The words came out harsher than she had intended. She softened her voice. "You don't have to be so formal when we're alone; I've told you a million times."

"But there are strangers among us, Eala," her sister protested. "We should keep the formality in check."

Eala sighed again. Deeper and louder. "Whatever you say, sister. You are my senior, after all." None of her siblings were true blood relations but were more of circumstantial kin, related by fate rather than genes. Still, she viewed them as her true brothers and sisters, and she respected their opinions and advice. "Cathal won't harm any of us, and as for the other one, he *will* be punished."

Laoise left the room, and for a moment, all she could hear was the sound of the birds outside and the rustling of the wind on the trees. She enjoyed the quiet, the sounds of nature around her; it soothed her. Her kind had been brought up in relative isolation, half the year at their small compound in the forests of the far north and the other half on the island. That was before her siblings and she had been brought down to Swan Island permanently to serve the king, the mighty monarch who thought himself to be more worthy of their care than the people they normally served. She didn't hate the island or the quiet life they led, but it bothered her that they had been denied their calling, that the world had been denied their service.

No point in such thoughts. She shook herself off, smoothed invisible wrinkles from her robes, and left her house. She'd visit the boy who had singlehandedly injured three of her swans. The boy reeked of evil as if instead of a soul, he carried around an empty core, one that could only be filled by wickedness and the pain of others. How could two brothers be so different? Cathal was gentle, caring, and she owed him her life. Not that she would ever tell him that. Let him think they didn't know each other; it would be easier to refuse his requests of mercy for his brother.

Odhran was curled up on a cot in the jail cell, a ten-by-ten space with no visible walls. The bars that held him prisoner were made of pure magic woven from the land and the skies around them. As soon as he saw her, he jumped to his feet and sneered. "Let me go," he demanded, no remorse in his voice.

She locked her hands in front of her. "What makes you think you deserve to be released?"

"I'm a mighty hunter, and I have more important things to do than sit here talking to a bunch of women." Spittle flew from his mouth as he stepped in her direction. "Let. Me. Go."

She turned and took a few slow steps to the side. "You injured several of my swans, *royal* swans," she said, never raising her voice. "Do you know what the sentence is for such an act?" He didn't say anything. "Death. Immediate execution." He winced. "You were lucky my people, rather than the king's guards, found you, or you'd be dead already."

He took another step toward the invisible wall. "You'll let me go then." It was not a question. He seemed to have already decided she was a push-over.

"I'm afraid that won't be possible, Odhran," she said, pausing her pacing to stare at him. "You've committed a crime, and you have to be severely punished." Anger flared in his eyes, and he lunged for the magic barrier. "I wouldn't do that if I were you. By now, you know how much it hurts when you touch it." The memory of the last time he had tried to escape must have resurfaced because he stopped mere inches from it. "Maybe I won't kill you. Maybe I will have your hands cut off. Then you won't be able to hunt ever again."

"You wouldn't dare," he said, blue eyes opening so wide, she thought they would pop.

"I would most definitely dare," she continued, ignoring his agitation. "Or maybe I'll poke your eyes out. That should keep you from going after innocent creatures."

"The swans' gizzards can cure the sick," he spewed, anger thick in each word. "Are you going to deny the sick from getting a cure in order to protect mere animals?"

Eala knew he was just grasping at straws, but his words struck a nerve. She was a Saintess, one of the holy healers whose life's calling was to help others; she couldn't condone the killing of the swans—the gizzard story was but a myth—but being on that island, at the mercy of a selfish king, prevented her and her siblings from curing the sick.

"Just free me, and I promise not to touch your precious birds," Odhran continued, his eyes narrowing. "I'll just leave."

"That won't do," she said, trying hard to control her anger toward the wicked boy. "You won't leave without punishment."

He began protesting, but she walked away, blocking her ears against his words. She felt no pity for Odhran, but her chest hurt when she thought of what Cathal would think when she told him his brother wouldn't be let go in one piece. Afraid she would give in to her wish to pay back Cathal's kindness, Eala sprinted all the way to the guards' quarters to tell them about the prisoner. Once the king's guards knew about him, there would be no going back. The boy would be punished.

EALA watched him from the doorway. Cathal lay on his back, his short raven hair in stark contrast with the white linen. For a brief moment, she wished things were different, that she didn't hold the fate of his brother in her hands, that they hadn't met under such circumstances. Then she shook her head, dispelling such foolish wishes. She was the queen and needed to uphold the law, especially those rules that protected her swans.

Despite her resolve, she had not reported it to the royal guards. Eala went as far as the guards' quarters, but as soon as she set eyes on the slacking men in various stages of dishevelment—some playing cards, some drinking, others slumped over tables fast asleep— she decided to wait a bit longer. The guards had grown complacent and lazy after years of no breach attempts. Who would be foolish enough to go against a royal order? Nothing but death would come of it, and yet, that cruel, misguided youth had thought he could get away with it. Even more unfortunate, he had brought his kind brother along for the ride.

She took a deep breath, rubbed her left shoulder, and stepped into the room. Cathal turned his head to her, first surprise and then a shadow of worry crossing his eyes. He tried to sit up but winced, and she quickened her step.

"Don't," she said, sitting on the edge of the bed. "Your injuries are still fresh. You may pop a stitch if you move too much." His well-shaped lips curved into a grimace of pain. She reached for him. "Let me help you."

Eale propped an extra pillow against the headboard and helped him move into a sitting position, tucking the sheets around his waist. He wore a plain white sleeping set, the top crisscrossed in front, allowing a peek at the bandages covering his chest.

"How's my brother?" Eala didn't know whether to admire him for his family loyalty or laugh at him for his misplaced worry. "Is he hurt?"

She folded her hands on her lap and restrained a scowl of disapproval. "He's fine. A lot better than he deserves." The sudden hurt in the man's face made her wish she hadn't said that, however true it was. "You do understand that he can't leave the island, right? Not alive anyway."

Pain shot in his eyes, clear and impossible to ignore. "I know he's cruel, but he's my brother. I promised my mother to take care of him after she died." He flattened his palm on his chest and coughed. "I can't break my promise."

Foolish man. "You can't, but I have made no such promise." Would he still look at her with friendly eyes once she punished Odhran? "I am truly sorry, but he wounded and tried to kill my swans. I think you know as well as I do, he will keep on killing other living creatures if we don't stop him."

Cathal hid his eyes under his thick lashes and hunched his shoulders. "May I see him?" he asked in a whisper.

How could she say no? She owed him her life. "When you recover a bit more," she said. He opened his mouth to protest, but she interrupted him, "I promise I won't punish him until you see him."

Cathal's tight shoulders relaxed. He raised his eyes to hers. "I'm worried about Mhamó," he said. "Is she doing all right?"

Eala smiled. "She's fine. I have one of my most promising young siblings taking care of her." Lily Pad was a bright young woman who was brave—or naive—enough to volunteer to go to Nem and watch over the old woman. "Lily Pad is an excellent healer and caretaker. Your grandmother will love her, I'm sure."

"Lily Pad?" Cathal's eyes opened wide. "Is that her real name?"

She couldn't help it; she repressed a chuckle with the back of her hand. "Nickname," she said. "It comes from her obsession with the plant. Every lily pad you see in our lake and ponds have been planted by her at some point in her life."

Laoise walked in on silent feet, carrying a tray. Cathal's gaze wandered to the woman whose lips were set in a tight line. Eala covered a smile with her hand; her sister did not approve of her care for the stranger and made no bones about showing it.

"Bring it here, Laoise," the queen said, gesturing to the small table by the bed. "Cathal, it's time to change the dressings covering your wounds."

Cathal stiffened visibly. Was he afraid of her? In the past few days, he had been unconscious while she treated him; thus, he had no way of knowing this wasn't the first time. "I can do it myself."

She smiled, and this time she made no attempt at hiding it. "Of course you can't. Unless your bones twist like no other human's does." She rolled up her long, sweeping sleeves. "I have been taking care of you since you got to the island. If I wanted to harm you, I would have done it already."

The queen soaked a piece of white cloth in the water and then turned to the other woman. "You can leave us, sister."

Laoise was not happy, but after a moment of hesitation, she obeyed, Cathal's gaze following her all the way out the door. "She doesn't like me." It wasn't a question.

She chuckled softly. "Laoise doesn't like strangers," Eala said, pulling down the sheets all the way to his hips to reach the ties on his shirt. "We don't get many visitors. It's normal for her to be suspicious. She means no harm."

His hand covered hers as she began untying the

straps that held the shirt closed. "What are you doing?"

"Isn't it obvious? I need to treat your wounds, and I can't do it through the fabric." She'd forgotten this was a man who was not used to being taken care of. He was the one caring for others. When had been the last time someone had shown any concern for him? "You're hurt, remember?"

Cathal's eyes were wide open as if he couldn't believe his own ears. "You're a queen. Why would you take care of me?"

Because you took care of me once. She couldn't tell him, and instead, she smiled. "Because of all my siblings, I am the one with the most skill." It wasn't a lie. There was a reason she was their queen, after all. She had been born a Saintess, her innate talents enhanced by years of specialized training only a few of her people had. But she had a personal interest in taking on Cathal's care, a debt of gratitude she was desperate to pay off.

He relaxed his hold on her hand and allowed her to untie and open his shirt. She couldn't believe how many scars he had across his chest, his abdomen, his shoulders. They continued in random patterns to his back. How had this man been hurt so many times? And why? She suspected his brother had a lot to do with it—another reason why she had to punish him. The boy had no heart if his own brother had to suffer that much to protect him.

Gently, she removed the bloody bandages from his

chest and began cleaning them with the wet cloth. Her swans had lacerated his skin and bruised several of his ribs. He was lucky no bones were broken, but he was still looking at a few weeks of healing before he could go back to his normal life. He cringed every time she swiped the cloth over his wounds but didn't complain. He was used to pain.

Grabbing a small pot of healing lotion, Eala looked up at him. Should she ask? "Why so many scars?"

"Life outside the island can be dangerous," he answered, evading the truth and her eyes. She opened the small pot and scooped a generous amount of the cream. "What's that?"

She stared at her cream-covered fingers. "This? Medicine. It will heal your wounds faster," she explained. "It won't hurt." As if to prove it, she began spreading it over his injuries. His muscles, tense mere moments ago, relaxed under her touch. She smiled. "It will also help with the pain."

Once she was done with his chest, she helped him turn around to repeat the treatment on his back. His back injuries were not nearly as severe as the ones on the rest of his body, but the old scars were deep and abundant. He had been whipped many times before.

After the treatment, she covered him up and cleaned the discarded bandages before standing up to leave. "Laoise will bring you some medicinal soup. After you eat, please rest. I will come again later."

Just as she turned to pick up the tray, he grabbed

her hand. "Thank you," he whispered. He was very pale. Eala would take him outside as soon as he was well enough to soak in some sunshine and the healing scents of nature. "Thank you for your kindness. I don't deserve it."

Eala straightened, tilting her head to the side. "Of course you do, Cathal. You deserve this and much more."

Not waiting to see his reaction to her cryptic words, she turned and left the room. If she wasn't careful, she would end up revealing things she would rather keep a secret from him. The less he knew, the easier it would be to decide what to do with his evil brother.

CHAPTER FIVE

Cathal

Damned if he'd stay in bed another minute. Cathal was not used to being idle; his life was a never-ending cycle of activity from the moment he opened his eyes at dawn until he could close them again at night. Taking care of his grandmother and keeping watch over his difficult brother was a full-time job on its own, but there was also the small garden to tend, eggs to carry to the landlords, and the odd jobs he was able to secure in town for extra income. The only downtime he had in the last few years was time spent in the dungeons because of something Odhran had done, and even he agreed that being beaten daily and eating rotten scraps didn't quite qualify as relaxing.

Getting out of bed was easier said than done; his whole body hurt, and his muscles and joints didn't seem likely to cooperate with his wish to move. Slowly, groaning under his breath, Cathal slid his long legs over the edge of the bed and moved into a sitting position. His chest burned, and he instinctively took a hand to it. He regretted it immediately as pain shot from the place he touched and radiated to his shoulder and arm. He bit back a scream and took long breaths to calm himself down. Despite the damage the swans had caused to his body, he couldn't blame them since they were merely defending their own.

After a few minutes, the pain subsided enough to attempt moving again. With deliberate slow movements, Cathal was able to stand, his legs barely holding his weight, and walk a few steps closer to a wall on which he could brace himself. Supported by the wall, he caught his breath, aware of every inch of aching flesh and sore joints. Who knew swans could be that vicious? He had been worried about the royal guards, never expecting to have to fight off birds instead.

The scent of flowers and spices filled his nose with each deep breath he took, soothing him. Cathal closed his eyes to better savor the sweet air. He wanted to see the island, that magical place surrounded by mystery and legend, kept as a precious jewel from everyone but the king. What secrets did it hold? He had dreamed about it often, especially since his brother had shot one of the swans all those years ago.

A few more labored steps, and he was at the

doorway. The door was kept open for most of the time he had been conscious, allowing the invigorating scented air to waft in with the breeze. He leaned against the door frame and sighed. It was even more beautiful than what he had imagined. Everywhere he looked, there were trees, some packed with colorful fruit, others exploding with delicate flowers. The cobblestone path meandered in between them, down a hill that seemed to end in a lake. He couldn't discern details from that distance, but the sunshine reflected off its surface, covering it in sparkling diamonds. The cacophony of bird songs competed with the cicadas and crickets. It was a festival for the senses that filled him with a feeling of something he couldn't identify at first but soon realized to be joy. It had been too long since he had felt it; he had almost forgotten it was possible.

"You shouldn't be out of bed." The stern voice startled him out of his reverie. Laoise stood a few feet away, her lips set in a thin line and her hands clasped in front. "You'll bust your stitches."

Cathal snorted. "Like you care if I do," he said, taking another long whiff of the sweetness around him. "You'd be happy if I died."

The woman harrumphed. "But my queen wouldn't, and I serve her, not my desires." At least, she was honest. He couldn't fault her for that. "Please, go back to bed." She moved closer to him and slipped a hand under his elbow. "I'll help you."

He didn't fight her. After seeing this amazing

island, he wanted nothing more than to heal quickly so he could explore it. Laoise led him to the bed and tucked the linens around his waist.

"Where's Eala?" he asked, accepting the cup of steaming tea the woman handed to him. The beautiful queen hadn't come to see him yet that day, an unusual enough occurrence to make him wonder. "Is something wrong?"

He could have sworn Laoise cringed as she quickly lowered her gaze to the floor. "Today is visiting day," she said, suddenly finding everything and anything on the floor interesting. "Our queen is visiting the king."

A sourness erupted in Cathal's tongue. What did that mean exactly? Was she one of the king's many concubines? King Rian had been married to a neighboring royal princess many years ago, but everyone knew he kept a harem which he frequently replenished with local young women. Was Eala one of them? Would a queen like herself submit to such a thing? He had known Eala for a very short time, and yet, the idea of another man touching her created waves of irrational anger inside him.

"For what?" The question flew out of his lips before he could stop it. It was not his place to ask, and the island people owed him nothing—much to the contrary, he owed them his life.

"It is our duty to minister to the king once a month," Laoise said, a touch of acid in her words. "Today is such a day."

"Do you all do it or just Eala?" And what exactly did she mean by minister? An invisible fist had closed around his heart.

Laoise looked at him then; her lips stretched so thin, he could barely see them. "You ask too many questions for someone who trespassed in the king's territory," she snapped. "You do realize that you are lucky to be alive, right? If it weren't for the kindness of our queen, you'd be long gone along with that monster you call your brother." She covered her mouth with a hand as if she had said something she wasn't supposed to. Before he could ask about Odhran, she turned on her heels and walked away. "Rest and stop asking questions. Eala will be back by tomorrow." He watched Laoise, her back straight as a rod, leaving the room.

This mystery, this magical aura around the island, and the swans had been a constant whispering as he grew up. People speculated by the hearth on long winter evenings and over market stalls during the summer, but Cathal had never paid it much attention, always too busy surviving to dwell on it. His mother, when her wits had still been with her, had told him tales of the magic swans, how a kiss from one of them could heal a dying man. Their mythical healing powers had caught the king's attention, his greed—not good news for the swans. Their freedom had since then been forfeited, shackled to the island forever in the service of the crown. But what about the people on the island? The beautiful queen who had never once been mentioned in the stories. Who was she? Who were these others she called siblings? And why was Eala *ministering* to the king?

Cathal shook his head and slid down under the sheets for a nap. What did it matter who they were or why they served the monarch? Where were his priorities lately? He had been muddled-brained since arriving at the island, but he had to focus—focus on recovering, rescuing his brother, and getting off the island. Whoever Eala and her people were was none of his concern, no matter how much those invisible strings tugged at his heart, no matter how tight his chest got when he thought of her with the king.

FOR a moment, he thought he was dreaming. Laoise stood before him with a strange chair on wheels, her lips turned into what might be a smile, and her arms crossed over her chest. Cathal stared at her first and then at the chair, not quite comprehending what it meant.

"I don't understand," he whispered, blinking his eyes rapidly; he was still not sure he was awake. "What's this for?"

The woman sighed loudly, her chest rising and

falling dramatically. "Are you daft, boy?" He hated being called that. He was hardly a child. In fact, he had never been a child, even when he was. He was nearly twenty-seven, and Laoise couldn't be more than a couple years older than him. "This is a wheelchair," she said, sweeping her hand in the air in a grand gesture. "It will allow you to move around the island without busting your stitches or re-injure your ribs."

"But—I thought—didn't you say?" he stuttered, unable to complete a coherent thought. "Am I free to move around?"

Laoise rolled her eyes and tapped her foot. "Why else would I bother to give you this chair? Unless you don't want it," she said, threatening to roll the chair away. "I can always take it back."

Cathal rushed to stop her, leaning forward on the bed and holding out his hand. "No, of course, I want it. I've been dying to see the outside. I just thought you didn't want me to."

She snorted. "I don't. But Eala does, and I obey my queen." She turned around to face the front door and yelled, "Padraig, get in here." A young man about Odhran's age walked in, dressed in white like Eala and Laoise normally dressed, a head froth with copper curls. "This is Cathal, your charge from now on." Cathal's chin dropped. "You are to take him wherever he wants to, except the forbidden areas, and keep him safe from danger." Danger for Cathal or the others?

The boy bowed his head and approached the bed.

"Would you like to go on a walk, Cathal?" he asked, offering his arm for support. Cathal nodded, still a bit stunned by the offer, and accepted his hand to slide out of bed and into the chair. Padraig snatched a coverlet from the bed and tucked it over Cathal's legs. "It might be a bit chilly outside."

Laoise, her lips back to the usual straight line, nodded in approval. "Remember, no shenanigans." Cathal couldn't be sure who she was talking to, him or the boy. Maybe to both. The red-haired youngster nodded and gave the chair a push in the direction of the door. "Be back by the evening."

Despite a chilly breeze, the weather outside was glorious; the sun shone brightly up in the sky with not a cloud in sight. Once again, Cathal took a deep breath to inhale the sweetness of the air, flowers, and fruit mingling together in a delicious and soothing scent.

"Where do you want to go first?" Padraig asked.

He didn't hesitate. "Down to the lake." That strip of sparkling blue had been on his mind since he'd seen it the day before. It called to him much the same way the ocean had always done. The little free time he had was often spent sitting on the sand or a rock and staring at the moving waters, dreaming of what might be beyond the horizon. Was there another place for him on the other side, one where he could be free, be himself? It was easy to dream when his senses were full of blue and salt, swayed by the waves and serenaded by the gulls. But the shackles of his life held him firmly in place, no matter how many times the wings of his wishful thinking tried to fly him away.

Padraig was young and slim but strong as he pushed and steered the heavy wheelchair down the cobbled path. Despite the speed with which the young man moved the chair, Cathal wanted to jump out of it and run. For once, he didn't have to take care of the garden or run errands in town or chase down his irresponsible brother. He could just enjoy the invigorating air and sight. He might have been injured and possibly stuck on the island, but he had never felt as free as he did at that moment.

With his heart racing alongside the wheelchair, Cathal finally arrived by the lake. He was dumbfounded by the sheer size of the body of water, which stretched as far as the eye could see in a satiny expanse of soothing blue. "Where does it end?" he asked in a whisper. Speaking loudly before such majesty seemed almost blasphemous.

"The lake?" The boy had a pleasant low voice, calm and mature, and Cathal couldn't help comparing it with his own brother's, which was the total opposite. "I'm not sure it ends. It's like a belt that holds the island together." Cathal raised his eyebrows, and the young man continued, "If you follow it, you'll end up here again."

Cathal reminded himself he was on a magical island where most things would be hard to understand and explain. He liked that. He enjoyed the irrational, imagination-fueled idea of Swan Island. His whole life had been steeped in harsh reality, interrupted only by brief moments of daydreaming, which, however short, were the glue that kept him together. Stories of fantastic beasts and magical creatures filled his head whenever life became too difficult to deal with. Unicorns and dragons had kept him company, if only in his head, in the long days and nights he languished in dungeons after whippings he didn't deserve. Memories of the magic swan he had taken care of for a couple of weeks years ago resurfaced. He wondered if the animal was on the island and if he would be able to see it. However exhausted he had been back then from lack of sleep, he had also been the happiest he could remember, his chronic loneliness assuaged by the quiet company of the beautiful creature. During those weeks, he had often fantasized the swan understood and talked to him. Fancies of a tired mind, he knew.

"Where are the swans?" He hadn't planned to ask, but with his mind full of memories of the wounded swan, the words escaped unbidden.

Padraig stumbled a step backward. He stuttered, "Wh-what do-do you mean?"

Surprised by the boy's reaction to such a simple question, Cathal hesitated. "The magical royal swans," he said, narrowing his eyes. "This is Swan Island, isn't it?"

An awkward and tense smile stretched across the young man's face. "Ah, yes, of course, the swans."

Cathal studied his companion, who seemed at a loss for words. "Well, they're—I mean, they're around here somewhere." Cathal tilted his head, his eyes narrowing further. "They're wild animals, and they come and go."

"Aren't your people their guardians?" What else would they be doing on the island? He had assumed that was their job. "How come you don't know where they are?"

Padraig lowered his eyes to his fidgeting hands. "We do take care of them, but we don't keep track of where they are."

It made no sense, but it was painfully obvious the boy was uncomfortable talking about it, so Cathal didn't press the matter and decided to enjoy the beauty of the lake instead. "Thank you for bringing me here, Padraig," he told his companion. "It's beautiful."

The boy's shoulders relaxed, and the forced smile on his face smoothed out into a genuine one as his eyes scanned the horizon. "Yes, it is magnificent," he said. "Like a liquid sky."

Cathal couldn't agree more with Padraig's assessment because even at night, when he sneaked out of bed to peer out the door, the lake looked as if it was studded with stars. Liquid sky indeed.

CHAPTER SIX

Gilded Cages

Eala

The sheets were cool and soft. Eala released a sigh. She could finally rest for the first time in days. Her monthly visits to the palace always left her drained and full of melancholy—a stern reminder of her lost freedom.

She turned on her side and closed her eyes only to reopen them a few seconds later, her head filled with images and thoughts of the life that had been but would never be again. She'd been a fool who had taken her own people down into that gilded cage she lived in now. Her naive and starry-eyed thoughts and actions had doomed herself and her siblings to a life of servitude. What was the use of being a queen and a magic healer if your life was not your own?

With a grunt, she flipped to the other side, her eyes

still wide open and her tired body refusing to relax. At least this visit was over. Tomorrow morning, after she recovered enough of her strength, she'd go back to the island and not have to see or hear from the king until the next scheduled visit. Eala had become an expert at locking those memories and worries away until she couldn't escape their reality anymore. She was able to ignore the fact that in another month, she'd be back at the palace, back in the king's bed, back to hating herself for what she had allowed herself and her people to become. Despite the weakness in her body, she had made herself linger in a hot, scented bath for almost an hour, soaking and scrubbing the pain and shame away. No matter how tired she was, Eala wouldn't go to bed with the king's scent on her skin, his taste in her mouth.

The next morning, dizzy with lack of sleep, Eala dressed and packed her medical bag, ignoring the lavish breakfast laid out for her at the table. The sooner she left, the quicker she could put this visit in that dark room in her brain. She strapped the small bag to her back and walked out onto the large balcony that faced the mountains. The city of Nem spread out in the valley below, hugged by the ocean and the rolling hills that grew into the White Mountains beyond. It was a beautiful sight with its dark red sloping roofs and contrasting flowers of almond and jacaranda trees; pity she couldn't fully enjoy it with the darkness which grew inside her each time she visited.

Eala took a deep cleansing breath, opened her

arms, and watched as her skin became covered in white feathers, one after another until her whole body didn't resemble a human any longer. Her lips stretched and puckered into a hard beak, and her toes became elongated and webbed. The metamorphosis used to be agonizing, but it barely registered anymore. She had become numb inside and out, incapable of feeling pain or joy. A mere husk of a woman who lived for one thing only: to protect her people from the cruel king who kept them captive.

TIRED from the long flight home and still a little unsteady on her human legs, Eala watched him as he slid off the chair after arguing with Padraig for a while. The boy had not been convinced at first, but eventually, Cathal convinced him he was strong enough to walk on his own. Maybe she should have stepped out from behind the trees and stopped him; he wasn't strong enough yet, after all. But she couldn't fault him for the obvious pleasure he derived from feeling the pebbles under his feet, the coolness of the water as he crouched to stick his hand in the lake, the softness of the breeze as it blew over his uplifted face. She had once felt like that—free and in perfect communion with nature—

so she didn't move, choosing to watch him from her hideout instead.

"Come here, Padraig," Cathal called, waving at the young man. "This water feels amazing."

Padraig hesitated for a moment but then did as he asked, lowering himself into a crouch by the water. "It's just water, Cathal," the boy said with a raised eyebrow.

Cathal chuckled. "Yes, it is, but water has a kind of magic. Did you know?" Eala sharpened her ears, her interest piqued. "Back home, when I think I can't deal with life anymore, I go to the beach and sink my feet in the wet sand and let the water talk me off of giving up on living."

The boy snorted, but Eala's breath caught in her throat. Was Cathal's life that bad that he had thought of ending it? Nevertheless, the boy sank his hand in the water and squealed in delight. "Cold," he said. Cathal laughed at the boy's reaction, scooped water in his palm, and splashed him. The boy jumped to his feet, squawking like a duck, a mixture of glee and outrage on his face.

It took Eala a moment to identify the growing stretch of her lips and the burgeoning bubble in her chest; she was smiling, a giggle fighting to escape her throat. It had been so long since she experienced any kind of joy, much less that sense of childlike, innocent delight.

The two males stopped laughing and looked in her direction. "Who's there?" Padraig asked, spinning on his heels. "Show yourself."

There was no point in hiding. Eala stepped around the trees and faced the two men. "Calm down, Padraig. It's just me."

The boy almost tripped over his feet to bow down to her. "My Queen," he exclaimed. "Sorry, I didn't see you."

She gestured him to straighten while her gaze moved to Cathal, who was right behind the boy, still crouched by the water's edge. He had gained some weight, and color had returned to his cheeks. Cathal was a handsome man, towering over her and even Padraig, with dark brown hair and sparkling brown eyes. As soon as their eyes locked, a generous and genuine smile spread across his face, and her heart fluttered. Not sure of what to make of it, Eala took her hand to her chest as if to control it. The smile vanished from her face, and heat rose to her neck and cheeks. What was wrong with her?

"Hi, Eala," Cathal said, stumbling a little as he stood up. Padraig rushed to his side to support and help him to the chair. "I was wondering where you were."

Still breathing too hard, Eala took a moment before speaking, "I trust Laoise treated you well."

He nodded, wiping his wet hand on his pants. "She did. No complaints," he said, his eyes never leaving hers. "Where were you?"

Anxiety filled her chest with wasps. "I was at the palace." Not a lie but not the whole truth either. "We should get him inside, Padraig. It's getting chilly." The breeze had indeed picked up, and the temperature had dropped enough that the skin on her arms puckered. When Cathal opened his mouth to protest, she cut him off, "If you get sick now, you will never recover."

She fully expected him to argue, but he didn't. Instead, he settled onto the chair and allowed Padraig to push him up the hill to the pavilion where he'd been staying. She followed them, a few steps behind where she could watch him without being noticed. She didn't believe in coincidences. The fact that they had met again after so many years had to mean something. But what exactly? He was a poor man, overly invested in a brother who did not deserve his love and care. A man who had trouble keeping his head above water. She remembered the stories he had told her every night for two weeks, stories of how he had been punished over and over again for things Odhran had done, of how Cathal had taken responsibility for the many crimes and sins of his younger brother. He was not someone who could rescue her people, who could bring their insufferable situation to an end. Cathal had no power other than his kindness and smile.

Padraig helped Cathal onto his bed and then excused himself. Eala stayed behind, the inexplicable need to talk to him gnawing at her. He raised his hazelnut eyes to her and smiled again. "Will you keep me company until Laoise comes with my dinner?"

She should have said no. She should have turned

around and left, but instead, she pulled a chair closer to the bed and sat down, her hands fidgeting on her lap. "She should be here with tea any minute," she said unnecessarily.

"Why do you go to the king?" Her breath caught. Cathal didn't seem to believe in beating around the bush. It was a quality she normally admired, but in this case, she'd prefer if he showed a bit more restraint. "No one would tell me."

Eala sighed. "That's because it's none of your concern." She hoped her tone was gentle. It wasn't as if it was a secret but rather a shame she carried around with her, a shadow that followed her everywhere she went. Even though she shouldn't have cared what he thought of her, she did. "It's a private matter between King Rian and me." Even uttering his name left a sour taste in her mouth. She controlled the urge to shudder and struggled to keep an impassive expression.

"Laoise said you were ministering to him." Cathal stubbornly pressed on. "What does that mean?" Why did he look angry? And why in the Guardians' name was he determined to find out?

Thankfully, Laoise walked in, effectively interrupting the conversation. "I have tea and pastries," she announced, raising her eyes and stopping suddenly as they met her queen. "I beg your pardon, Your Majesty. I didn't know you were here."

"I came to visit our guest, but I should probably be going." She made as to get up, but Cathal's hand shot out to hold her in place. She stared at his hand, closed around her wrist, firm but gentle. "I have business to take care of."

"Stay a while," he begged. Then he lowered his voice to a whisper, "I won't ask about the king, I promise." She nodded and relaxed. He still held her. "Drink some tea with me. Please."

She gave in and stayed. He kept his promise and never once asked about her visits to the royal palace. But he hadn't promised not to bring up his brother, so he did. Somehow making excuses about Odhran, who would not have a good ending, was a lot more comfortable than talking about the king. She told him what she knew, which was not much; he would be punished, but she didn't know how or when yet. He would most definitely pay for his crimes, though.

CATHAL'S usually gentle eyes had hardened into true ambers, hard and cold. Eala felt the ice of his glare run through her, down her spine to her toes. She swallowed hard, struggling to keep her composure but mostly to stop herself from giving in to his request. However difficult, she held his gaze with her own and didn't allow the trepidation in her heart to show.

"Your brother is our prisoner—a dangerous one at that," she said, keeping her voice level and low. "I cannot risk it."

His lips were squeezed together so tightly, they had turned almost white, but when he opened his mouth to speak, color came flooding in, filling every inch of his full lips. His well-shaped jaw and upper lip were partially covered in dark stubble, but she couldn't miss the tightening of his muscles below them.

"All I'm asking is to see him," he growled from between his teeth. "I'm not going to help him escape. I just want to see him, that's all."

Eala was not sure what she feared the most if she gave in to him: hurting him or having him hate her. Odhran was not in the best of shape. They fed him but denied him all other comforts. After all, he was lucky to still be alive. He was a psychopath and didn't deserve their mercy. But she couldn't bring herself to execute him—not that she felt sorry for him, but because she didn't want to hurt Cathal. Cathal deserved better, but like her and her people, he'd been dealt a terrible hand, and she didn't want to make it worse.

She took a deep breath. "Cathal, please be reasonable. Your brother nearly killed several of the swans." And herself all those years back. She clearly remembered Cathal apologizing for his brother when he came to care for her. The boy was a monster.

His eyes suddenly softened and shone. "Please, I want to see him one last time." Turns out, he knew. He knew Odhran would be executed sooner or later. The ice in her heart began to thaw. She couldn't deny him a last goodbye, could she?

She waved Laoise closer. "Get things ready," Eala told her, a knot in her throat making it difficult to speak. "I will take our guest to see his brother."

Laoise stiffened, and her lips twitched in disapproval. Or maybe it was worry. She knew as well as her queen that Odhran should have been dealt with a long time ago and that if the king found out he was still alive and now receiving visitors, they would all be in trouble. Yet, Eala knew her sister would never disobey her, and Laoise knew exactly what to do to make this visit as secret and safe as possible. Laoise mumbled a reluctant acknowledgment, bowed briefly, and left the room.

Cathal's face was opened into a smile that brightened the space. Eala swallowed hard again. What was about this man that made her feel as if every inch of her body was on pins and needles? Not a totally unpleasant feeling but unsettling. She wasn't used to feeling unbalanced.

"I will check your wounds first," she said, covering her discomfort with the mask of practicality. "Then I will take you to his cell." Cathal's cheeks flushed, and she could have sworn his eyes twinkled like the true gems they were. "Take off your clothes." Heat climbed her neck, invading her face all the way to the roots of her hair as she realized what she had said.

A tiny smile danced on his lips as Cathal gingerly removed his crisscross white top. Flustered, she watched as he bared his scarred but well-muscled chest and shoulders to her. Breaking from the semi-freeze, Eala turned her back on him and busied her hands and thoughts with the medical kit on the table. When she finally spun around, her guest had fully stripped off his shirt and sat on his bed in glorious upper body nakedness. Much to her mortification, Eala gulped but couldn't move her gaze away from the scarce fuzz that covered his lean, strong chest.

He was beautiful. Even with skin marred by scars of all sizes and shapes, his good looks shone through, and she couldn't stop wondering whether they were a mere reflection of his inner beauty—his kindness and generosity.

Slowly, she closed the space between them and sat on the edge of the bed. Eala gently began uncovering his wounds, making herself focus on the movement of her fingers and not on his chest as it rose and fell with his breath.

"This may hurt a little," she said, discarding the soiled bandages on a nearby pail. Most of the injuries were healing nicely, covered by new skin already, but one on the flat of his left shoulder still sported an angry red color. She patted the wet towel around its edges, cleaning and studying it. He winced. "Sorry. This one looks infected still."

"I'm used to it," he said with a chuckle. She glanced

up from his wound, failing to see the humor in it. He had so many scars, you'd think he was a warrior. "Life is complicated in Nem." Like that explained everything.

She lowered her eyes again, continuing to clean the lesion. "You should never have to be punished for your brother's bad choices." She bit her tongue, afraid she'd said too much.

"How do you know that's what happened?" he asked, narrowing his eyes.

Eala didn't look up and dipped a long cotton swab in antiseptic. "I guessed right, didn't I?" It was better if he didn't know yet. "I can tell you dote on Odhran, but he doesn't deserve your protection and loyalty." Now that she was talking, she couldn't stop. She dabbed the disinfectant on the angry wound. "Given the chance, he would leave you out to die to save his neck."

She felt him stiffen under her fingers, and she chided herself silently for having said too much, for sticking her nose where it didn't belong. He didn't say anything else, and she finished dressing the wound in silence, the tension between them palpable, a wall he had erected. Little did he know that, like him, Eala had been kept in a cage for years.

Laoise came back soon after Cathal donned his shirt once again, silence still heavy in the room. The woman's gaze ping-ponged between Eala and Cathal, undoubtedly sensing the awkwardness. "Everything's ready, my Queen," she said, not bothering to bow. "Should I take him to the cells?"

Eala shook her head and stood up. "No, I will take him myself." She hadn't known Cathal for long, and yet, she knew how soft-hearted and loyal he was; all his brother had to do was say the right words, and she didn't doubt for a minute that Cathal would risk everything to rescue Odhran. She had to protect Cathal and her people. If Odhran was released, he would most likely go on a rampage and kill as many swans as he could. She had covered it up once; she couldn't do it again.

Cathal got on his feet, and she gestured for Laoise to bring him a cloak. The sun was setting, and the breeze had cooled down enough that he'd need it. He accepted it, however reluctantly, still refusing to say anything.

"Let's go see your brother," Eala said. Coming to a decision, she added, "If I were you, I'd say my goodbyes. Odhran will be punished very soon." Eala didn't stop to see his reaction; she knew it would hurt to see the pain in his eyes.

CHAPTER SEVEN

Odhran

Cathal

She was avoiding his gaze. Every time Cathal sped up to catch up with her, she did it too, as if determined to walk ahead of him. Despite the coldness of her demeanor, he knew there was warmth beneath. Compassion. Otherwise, why would she take care of him for the past few weeks when he was a trespasser on her sacred island? But for whatever reason, Eala stubbornly stuck to her icy attitude even when sadness or sympathy softened her blue-green eyes. He had to figure out a way to make her change her mind about his brother. Cathal agreed that Odhran needed to be punished, but the thought of death made him turn cold inside and out. From beyond the grave, his mother yelled at him in his dreams, reminding him of the deathbed promise he'd made to always protect Odhran no matter what.

"You must protect him at all costs. He's special," Mom had said time and time again.

Odhran was indeed special, but not in a good way. Cathal knew that mothers will love even their undeserving children, but he had never quite understood why his mom had been so insistent on treating his wild and cruel brother as a jewel the world could not afford to lose. His birth was shrouded in mystery; to this day, Cathal couldn't recall his mother's pregnancy. He had already been ten when Odhran was born, but he couldn't conjure up images of his mom swollen with child. There was a vague memory of her coming back with a crying bundle in her hands after a short absence. Even then, Odhran had been a difficult child, crying nonstop and keeping them all up at night, but his mom doted on the fussy baby, singing him softly to sleep even when she was so sick, she could barely move.

"Now that your mother is gone, Cathal, you must not forget your oath to her," his grandmother had said the day they buried his mom. His heart had been twisted into a tight knot, aching and bleeding from the loss of the one person who loved him. The last thing he wanted to think about was of how to protect a kid brother who didn't bother to shed a tear. Mhamó was right, though; he had promised, and he always kept his promises.

"Why must I protect him, Mhamó?" he had asked, tears still trailing down his cheeks. "What's so special about my brother?"

Grandma had looked away and sighed. "One day, you'll find out, child," she'd whispered, her gaze lingering on the fresh dirt of his mother's grave. "Until then, keep him safe and alive. Your own life might depend on it."

Cathal had a million questions, but grief had overwhelmed his childish heart, and for years after the funeral, he did exactly what he promised, no questions asked. But that nagging curiosity was back now that his brother had committed a capital crime and his death seemed inevitable. He loved his brother, but he certainly didn't like him and couldn't in clear conscience condone the things Odhran had done.

Eala stopped abruptly, and Cathal locked the wheels of the chair so as not to crash into her. They were standing before a large dome-roofed, circular building. Other than its shape, nothing marked it as different from the others on the island. It had a light brown wooden facade punctured by square shuttered windows and a massive wooden double door. He scanned the structure with curiosity. Was this where his brother was being kept? It didn't seem remotely as dank as the places where Cathal had been imprisoned, redeeming for his brother's evil acts.

"Can you walk?" Eala asked without turning to face him. There were a few steps up to the entrance and no visible ramps that would allow his wheelchair access.

He nodded. He could walk just fine; the reason he was still in the chair was that Eala wouldn't have it any other way. He slid off the chair, trying out his legs, weakened from lack of use. A little unsteady, Cathal took a few steps toward her, strength returning with each movement. It felt good to walk on his own two legs.

When he stopped beside her, she finally looked at him. "Are you sure you want to do this?" she asked, her face set in ice. "It won't be easy for you, and your brother is a master at manipulation. He'll try everything to make you break the rules and help him."

Cathal's stomach clenched. She was right; his brother had always been able to get what he wanted from him, and now that his life was at risk, he would give it all he had. His will wavered for a moment, but then the memory of his promise replaced his hesitance. "I'm sure."

Without another word, Eala led him up the stairs. When Cathal stumbled, his legs still wobbly, she took a step back and placed a hand under his elbow to support him. He breathed a thank you and accepted her help, blushing at how her touch made his heart flutter.

Just like on the outside, the inside of the building was not what Cathal would ever suspect to be a prison. There were very few furnishings: a few chairs and tables along the curved walls, painted clay figurines of the Guardians in niches carved from the wood, and a startling white swan-shaped statue carved from what looked like marble sitting on the top of a stone pedestal. Eala left him standing by the entrance and strode toward the swan after a couple of brief bows to the Guardians on either side. Without hesitation, she placed her hands on the swan's wings and twisted them.

Cathal's jaw dropped. The statue turned at her command, and a loud mechanical noise echoed through the space.

Eala stepped back as half the floor beneath the pedestal cracked and swung open into a square hole. Eala turned her head to him and waved her fingers. "Come," she said simply.

He followed her quietly, not sure what to expect as they went down a steep and narrow staircase lit by torches. What was this place? Had she finally had enough of him and decided to kill him? Or was this where she was keeping his brother?

The stairs leveled into a long, wide corridor that seemed as if carved off a large slab of gray stone. Despite the many torches hanging along the walls, the place was dim and gloomy, but as they approached the end, a strange glow spread on the floors. As soon as they went around the bend, Cathal saw where it was emanating from; the corridor widened into a large circular room dominated by a dome of unnatural yellowish light. The glow formed a wall of energy that, however transparent, looked as solid as rock. Within its confines, Cathal spotted a familiar seated figure, his blond, scraggly hair falling over his eyes.

"Odhran!" Cathal exclaimed.

The boy whipped his chin up, and his blue eyes met his brother's. Anger quickly replaced the surprise reflected there. "Cathal? You're alive?" Odhran stood and took a few steps closer to the wall of light separating him from Cathal and Eala. "Are you in cahoots with this bitch?" The words were spat rather than spoken.

Cathal winced. "Don't speak about our hostess that way, boy," he told his brother with no expectations of being obeyed. "Your life is in her hands, and you're lucky to still be alive."

Odhran's lips twisted into a sneer. "You've always been a weakling, my brother, both physically and in mind." Cathal should have been offended, but the truth was he was used to his brother's scorn. "Do you think she'll spare your life after taking mine? Think again, Cathal. If you don't get us out of this place, she'll kill us both."

Suddenly, Cathal wanted to lay down, forget he had a brother, forget everything, and just sleep. He sighed and turned to Eala. "May I speak to him alone, please?" Not because he was planning on anything secret, but it was hard to swallow being talked to like that by his brother in front of her. What would she think of him, seeing how he took such treatment from a kid brother?

She thought for a moment before answering, "Ten minutes, not a minute more." She turned to leave but stopped and told Odhran, "Don't get any ideas, boy.

You are not getting off of this island alive." And she left.

AS soon as Eala had left the room, Odhran crossed his arms over his chest and smirked. "She has you wrapped around her little finger, doesn't she?" he said, clicking his tongue. "You don't get laid enough, brother. Get yourself a woman, and you won't be vulnerable to bitches like her."

Anger and revulsion erupted inside Cathal. "Eala is not a bitch, Odhran. You should thank her for the fact that you are still here talking to me." Exhaustion made him heavy as if the stone floor beneath him could swallow him whole at any time. "By law, you should have been executed the moment you set foot on this island. You even shot the swans." New anger fed the fire in his chest. "How could you be so stupid, so reckless? Those are the king's swans, sacred animals that no one is allowed to touch."

His brother shrugged. "How would he ever find out who killed them?" he sneered, dropping to the floor and crossing his legs. "If I had been successful, I would be rich. The swans' gizzards can cure all sorts of diseases."

Cathal sighed, brushing a palm over his face. "Those are myths, brother. There is no proof that those stories have an ounce of truth to them."

Odhran's eyes lit up, the corner of his lips kicking upward. "Oh yeah? Have you noticed how the old king never ages?" It was true that the king who should be in his fifties never looked a day older than thirty, but it couldn't possibly have anything to do with the swans. "You've never heard the rumor that the swans' kiss can keep you young forever?"

Despite the situation, Cathal burst out laughing. How ridiculous was that story? "Are you suggesting our king has been making out with birds?" As depraved as the monarch was rumored to be, Cathal couldn't believe for a moment he would stoop to bestiality to keep himself young.

"Go on, laugh," his brother said, leaning back on his arms casually. "The story goes that every month a swan is taken to the palace to—how did they put it?— serve the king." Laughter died on Cathal's lips. "What do you think that entails? Playing catch? Serving food? Or fucking him?"

Cathal shook his head. No, it was too sick, too— his mind couldn't even conceptualize such a thing. It couldn't be true, could it? He had heard of men copulating with animals, but his king? "Stop being so blasphemous, Odhran. When are you going to grow up and be the man Mom thought you could be?"

"Mom lived with her head in the clouds," Odhran spat out, anger shining in his eyes. "And that's why she died. If she had been smart, she'd still be alive."

Red clouded Cathal's vision. How dare he talk about their mother like that? He advanced toward his brother, his hand above his head, closed into a fist and oblivious to the curtain of light between them.

"I wouldn't do that if I were you," his brother cooed, mischief dancing in his eyes. "That invisible wall carries a serious punch. Trust me, I've tried."

Stopping right before touching the light, Cathal dropped his hand slowly, breathless. "How can you speak of your own mother like that?"

"I don't remember her well, but from what Mhamó told me, she was dumb and naive," Odhran continued, no remorse in his voice. "It was probably a good thing she died when she did."

Why was he here, trying to save this horrible person's life? Odhran might be his blood brother, but he was nothing like Cathal and didn't deserve the care his mother had given him. Cathal spun around and began walking away.

"Hey, where are you going, brother?" Odhran yelled out.

"I'm leaving and never coming back," Cathal said, not bothering to turn around. "Do not call me brother."

Cathal heard some scuffling, and then his brother said, "Wait, I'm sorry. I'm just angry. Don't go. Please."

Despite knowing that the change in his brother's

tune was nothing but a ploy to keep him there, Cathal stopped and turned around again. "Why should I stay?"

Odhran was standing now, the smirk off his face. He looked younger somehow and vulnerable. "Because you're my brother, and I need you." Cathal stared in silence. What could Odhran do that he hadn't done already? "You have to get me out of here, brother. They are going to kill me."

Cathal lowered his eyes. Yes, they would kill him sooner or later. "I don't know what to do. I've been trying to convince Eala to let you go, but you caused such injuries."

"Come after midnight," his brother said suddenly, lowering his voice to a whisper. "They switch the guard and leave the gate open for a short time. I've been watching them; I know how to turn off the screen of light."

His heart skipped a beat. "I can't do that," Cathal whispered. "I can't betray Eala's trust."

Odhran's face hardened. "Who's your kin? Me or that bitch?" He stomped a foot, and dirt puffed around him. "She's nothing to you. Nothing! What do you care if you betray her? What about your own brother?"

Cathal shook his head, not believing what his brother was suggesting. Truth be told, he didn't see a way out either; Eala was determined to punish Odhran for his crime, and Cathal couldn't just stand and watch his brother die. But he couldn't stand the idea of betraying Eala either. His brother might think she was nothing to him, but that wasn't true; she was something. In fact, in the past couple of weeks, she had turned into much more than that.

Eala was now everything.

As if guessing his thoughts, Odhran exploded in laughter. "Oh, my Guardians, I can't believe it; you're all hot for the queen of the bitches."

"Shut up." Heat burned Cathal's neck and cheeks. Was it possible? Had he fallen in love with the beautiful and enigmatic queen?

"Remember, brothers before whores." His brother's words soured in his stomach. If Odhran was trying to convince Cathal to set him free, he wasn't doing a great job by insulting the woman Cathal respected more than anyone else in the world. "You have to snap out of it. Once we go back to Nem, I will buy you the sexiest whore in town, but you have to get me out of here now."

"You should go for it, Cathal." Eala's voice came from behind him, surprising even his brother into silence. "That sounds like an amazing offer: risk your head to save him, and he will get you laid. Fair trade, I suppose."

If his face had been burning before, it was now a tundra fire. "Eala, I didn't hear you coming."

She moved with the grace of a dancer, her white clothes flowing like water around her. "Neither did your brother," she said, her voice a rich caramel. "Are you sure you share the same genes? He's nothing like you."

It was not really a question, so Cathal didn't answer. Eala stared at Odhran, who was now shooting fire with his eyes. "I'm hoping that your brother is smart enough to see through your lies. You have done nothing but evil all your life. Why is that? Is your heart that hard and shriveled, you can't tell right from wrong?"

"I shot a few swans. How is that evil?" Cathal cringed. Even now, his brother didn't show any wisdom or sense of remorse. "They are only stupid birds. No one would miss them."

Eala went rigid. "I would miss them." Icy words brimmed with threat. "The visit is over, Cathal. Let's go."

Cathal threw a last glance at his brother before following her out of the cell and into the corridor, which took them to the stairs. Odhran's screams followed them all the way.

"I'm sorry for what he said," Cathal said, struggling to keep in time with Eala's steps. "He's always been a little rough around the edges."

She stopped abruptly and stared at him, eyes burrowing into his soul—eyes that could be as soft as feathers or as hard as stones. "He's not rough around the edges, Cathal. You need to open your eyes and accept that your sibling is a monster. The quicker you accept that, the best for you and everyone who has ever been hurt by his actions."

There was truth in her words, but the promise he had made his mother still haunted him, still pushed him in directions he didn't want to go…that he didn't think he should.

"Why do you protect him, Cathal?" Eala asked him.

"Because my mother asked me to," he admitted. "Before she died, she made me promise."

Her green eyes softened. "Didn't your mother want you to be happy?"

Cathal had asked himself that many times. Because of his promise, he did nothing except work and clean up after his brother. He never had a relationship that lasted longer than a roll in the back of an abandoned hut, and the only time he remembered not feeling completely alone was when he had cared for the wounded swan many years ago.

He shook his head and shrugged. "I don't know why she made me promise. She died before she could tell me. But she insisted he was very important and that one day he would be worth his weight in gold." Cathal sighed and stared at his own hands. "Mother had a lot of hallucinations toward the end of her life. Not even Mhamó with her knowledge of herbs could make her better."

A warmth on his forearm made him look up at her. Eala had closed her small hand around his wrist, making his heart gallop like a wild horse. "I'm sorry, Cathal. I'm so sorry you had such a tough life."

Her touch was playing havoc with his senses, and at least, for that moment, nothing else mattered—his mother, his brother, the king—there were only Eala and him connected by that small patch of skin.

The words were out of his mouth before he could stop them. "It was all worth it so I could meet you."

ODHRAN'S words swam in his mind, head-butting the edges of his memory. Something about what his brother had said made Cathal's heart jump to his throat, but what was it exactly? Something had triggered a—what? A memory? A connection?

Cathal tossed and turned in bed every night after the visit to his brother, conflicting feelings making it hard to breathe. What should he do? Allow Eala and her people to execute Odhran or betray her and try to free his brother? He'd have to be stupid to think he could get away with breaking his brother free from his cell. Even if he could walk in unspotted, the change of the guard only lasted a few minutes, and the time it took to walk to the cell and back would throw him and Odhran right into the guards' hands. Despite knowing this, he still considered it, the ever-gnawing guilt not letting go.

Padraig brought him breakfast and helped him get dressed for their morning stroll. Eala had finally allowed him to walk part of the way, now that even the most stubborn wound on his chest seemed to be on the mend. He would never admit it, but he still got tired easily even when they walked downhill. The protesting he always enacted once Padraig ordered him back on the chair was only for show; the reality was that his legs and his lungs welcomed the respite.

The lake shimmered in the sun as it always did, bringing serenity to the upheaval in his heart. He took his shoes off and sat on the edge of the water with his legs dangling over it while the boy collected herbs and flowers for his queen. With a hand over the throbbing chest scar, Cathal surveyed the large lake, squinting against the sunlight. He wished he could stay here forever. But his responsibilities called him; even if his brother didn't make it off of this island alive, he still had his grandmother to think of. Eala had promised she was being taken care of, but he couldn't help but worry.

A blur of movement behind some reeds that stuck out of the water a few feet away caught his eye. Was it a turtle, maybe? He had seen many on his daily excursions. Couldn't be a fox since it was too far from the bank. He narrowed his eyes, zooming in on whatever was moving in the water. He saw a flash of white—not a turtle then—and then a long, graceful neck.

A swan!

Cathal opened his mouth to call Padraig but didn't

utter a word, afraid he would spook the large bird. He had been on the island for a few weeks and had yet to see the sacred animals that inhabited it. An irrational part of him wondered whether that was the swan he had taken care of ten years ago. The animal swam into full view, his glorious white plumage in stark contrast with the deep blue of the lake. Cathal sighed.

"Are you okay?" Padraig asked, lifting his head to look at him.

The swan turned his beak in their direction but continued his languorous swim.

"A swan," Cathal said, feeling childish and stupid. What grownup would be so entranced by the sight of a bird?

The boy glanced toward the swan and smiled. "That's Fionn," he said with a wave. Then, he stopped and turned beet red. "We've named them all," he added awkwardly.

"How many are there?" Cathal asked, wondering how the boy could tell the swan apart from the others.

"Twelve," Padraig said, letting the last syllable fall. "At last count. There could be more."

The swan moved away until it became a mere white spot on the horizon. "How are the swans my brother hurt?"

"Healed for the most part," the boy said. He pointed at the vanishing whiteness. "That's one of them."

Relief flooded him. He didn't think he could handle the guilt if any of them had died. "That's good," he murmured, watching the pale spot getting smaller and smaller. His toes touched the cool water, and a sudden yearning assailed him. "Can you swim in this lake?"

Padraig snapped a twig in his hand and looked at him again, an eyebrow arched in surprise. "Yes, but it's cold."

Cathal stood and began undressing with a chuckle. "I have lived in the cold my whole life," he said, undoing the ties of his crisscross shirt. "This weather is positively balmy."

At first, the boy simply stared, paralyzed as Cathal peeled layers of clothing one at a time, the garments flying and falling around him on the grass, some snagging on nearby bushes like strange blooms. After a moment or two, Padraig burst out laughing and dropped the bag of herbs by his feet. "You're crazy," he said with a chuckle. "You're going to freeze."

Cathal was doubtful that he would be cold. The temperature of the water was mild at best, much warmer than the ocean waves he often bathed in. Water had always been as soothing for his body as it was for his mind. He loved the ocean like some people loved tea or chocolate; instead of ingesting it with his mouth, he inhaled it with his lungs and absorbed it through his skin. Since the salty, wild waters of an ocean were not available, the serene ones of the lake would do nicely.

Undressed all the way down to his thin white pants, Cathal leaned over the bank, glancing back at his companion. "Are you coming?"

Padraig laughed again and began disrobing. "You don't have to ask me twice."

Cathal didn't wait. Flexing his knees, he propelled himself into the air and dove head-first into the calm waters. The world went quiet as the waters enveloped him wholly. He had half expected the waters to be murky like in many lakes but found out they were crystalline instead. Everything under the water was sharply defined and clear as if seen through a magnifying lens. Small fish rushed past him in a rainbow of glittering scales, and a turtle swam close, its head stretching upwards as if asking, "Who is this crazy creature?"

He stayed beneath the waters for as long as his lungs could handle it and then swam up to the top, wondering where Padraig was. As soon as his head broke the surface, he saw the boy, sitting half-dressed on the grass and appearing contrite. Next to him, Eala stood, beautiful and intimidating, her well-shaped eyebrows knitted together and her arms crossed over her small breasts.

"Aren't you joining, Padraig?" he asked, knowing all too well what the answer would be. It seemed as if he had inadvertently gotten the boy in trouble with the queen. "The water feels heavenly," he felt the need to add.

"Padraig cannot be cavorting in the waters of the lake during his workday," she said. Cathal heard something she wasn't telling—a secret, the real reason she wouldn't let the boy swim with him.

The joy that swimming brought to him emboldened him. "Why are you cranky? Do you even know how to have fun?"

Padraig's eyes opened so wide, his eyeballs looked as if they were about to pop out. Eala didn't even blink. He had to give it to her; she was one cool cookie. "I know how to have fun, but I also know when it is not the time."

Recklessness pulled at him. "Are you working right now, my Queen?" She shook her head, and he added, "Why not join me then?" He gestured to the water in an invitation. "Or are you afraid you may not be able to handle the fun?"

There was silence for a moment while Eala stood still, her expression never changing except for the tiny, telling quirk of her lips. He was about to give up when she began unwrapping her outside robes. "Not that I need to prove myself to you," she said. "But the water does look amazing."

The boy's mouth had dropped open in awe as he watched his queen undressing all the way to her undergarments, the white silk embroidered diamond doudou that covered her breasts and the long flowing pants under her dress. Cathal watched her too, half in surprise and half in delight. He liked this adventurous, playful side of the beautiful woman who seemed too serious and somber all the time.

She plunged into the cool waters a few feet away from him and didn't resurface. He waited a few seconds and then, in irrational panic, dove after her. She wasn't too far from him, suspended by the gravity of the water, her red curls floating around and over her head, the thin fabric of her pants blowing up like balloons. He froze, bubbles releasing from his lips and floating to the surface as he feasted his eyes on the beautiful woman before him. Her ivory white skin, speckled with freckles, appeared even more flawless in the otherworldly light of the lake, and her full, perfectly bow-shaped lips were curved into a rare smile. His heart almost stopped.

After a moment, Eala pointed to the surface, reminding him that he needed to replenish his oxygen. They broke the surface at the same time, water splashing to all sides as they shook their heads and let out a bubbling of laughter. The queen knew how to have fun, after all.

They swam together until Eala headed to the bank. "I have to go," she said. "I don't spend my days idle like my guests."

It was said in obvious jest, but Cathal felt the sting of familiar guilt. He wasn't used to not doing anything. "I can work," he blurted out. Eala, hands braced to pull herself up onto the grass, froze for a moment. "Give me something to do, please. I'm recovered, and I can help."

The queen hesitated for a moment and then pulled herself up on land. "I will think about it," she promised, squeezing water from her hair. The fabric of the silk chest cover clung to her graceful curves, revealing and enticing.

He gulped, happy he was still underwater and she couldn't see how her beauty affected him. "I'll do anything: cleaning, cooking, picking up horse shit…" Eala and Padraig, who stood behind her, chuckled at the same time. Cathal's cheeks heated. "I'm used to it."

With the grace of a swan, Eala got up, her pants hiding little of her body beneath. She was still smiling. "I will send Laoise to you with lunch and a job assignment."

He nodded, his lips stretching in pleasure. "Thank you."

She turned around. "Padraig, make sure to dry him out. We don't want him sick now." The boy bowed and started collecting Cathal's clothes.

Eala began her walk back, so Cathal pulled himself out of the water and sat on the grass, waiting for the boy to bring him his dry clothes. When he looked up to watch Eala on the path, he stilled at what he saw on the back of her shoulder: a tiny tattoo of the Virgo constellation. He jumped to his feet and cleared the space between them in two strides.

"Wait!" he yelled out. Eala stopped, and he slowed down, taking his time with the last couple steps until he was right behind her. "Wait, please," he repeated in a whisper now. He lifted his hand and brushed his fingers over her tattoo. "I've seen this before," he murmured, his eyes following the movement of his fingers as he outlined the star formation on her skin. "I've seen this on one of your swans, Eala."

CHAPTER EIGHT

Memories

Eala

Eala wouldn't be surprised to find a rut carved into the marble floor of her room. She must have paced that floor for hours. After coming back from the lake, her mind and heart were lit with emotions she hadn't felt in years and, if, on the one hand, it made her feel alive again, it also worried her. She had schooled herself not to feel, not to allow anything to blur her one and only goal—to keep her people safe.

She should be worried Cathal had recognized her tattoo, getting that much closer to uncovering her secret, but all she could really think about was how his fingers had felt on her wet skin, a fluttery touch that set her on fire and muddled her thoughts. She had dismissed the tattoo the best she could think of at the time but wasn't sure he had bought it. Time would tell, she guessed. Despite everything, she couldn't help feeling an exhilaration she barely recognized; it had been too long since she'd had fun, since she'd smiled and laughed with gusto.

She sat on the edge of her bed, her nightclothes cool against her tingling body. She could still feel the water against her skin, the sun on her face, the feeling of floating in the water.

Cathal's eyes on her.

A shiver ran down her spine, and she hugged herself. "You're not a girl anymore, Eala," she said, slipping under the covers and adjusting the pillow under her head. "The time to be foolish and vain has long gone. Snap out of it."

Sleep didn't come easy. In her head, she replayed the events of that day, how wonderful and alive she had felt diving into the lake, not worried about what terrible thing might happen. Granted, she had done it at first to prevent Padraig from getting in the water; he was young and still inexperienced. He might not have been able to control the urge to shift, exposing their secret to their guest. In the end, it was her tattoo that almost gave them away.

"Would it be so bad?" she mumbled, pulling the sheets up to her chin. "Would it really be terrible if Cathal knew our secret? He's a good man, kind, generous, and honest. He'd keep the secret; I know he would." But it wasn't her secret alone, and she had no right to break her people's trust.

She tossed to her side, irritated with herself for the restlessness that kept her awake. Too lost in thought, she almost missed a light knocking at the door. Who could that be? It was late. The others would have all retired to their rooms by now, and the guards didn't dare come close to their side of the island without being invited. They knew the king would behead them if they did.

"Who's there?" she yelled out, sitting up on the bed.

"It's me, Cathal." Her heart did a flip. "May I come in for a moment, please?"

What could he possibly want? It was the first time he had ever come to her quarters in the biggest building on the island. Biggest, not because it was the queen's, but because it doubled up as a meeting hall for the others and where they often ate together.

"Come in," she said, pulling the covers tightly across her lap. Her red hair fell loosely over her shoulders, a flame against the snow of her sleeping garments.

Cathal walked in, dressed like her in the white nightclothes they all wore, his crisscross shirt revealing his strong neck from where a small stone amulet hung and fell over his chest. He shut the door behind him and closed the space between them in two strides. "Sorry to bother you so late, my Queen," he said, standing awkwardly a few feet from the bed.

"We're alone. Call me Eala." Her throaty voice

seemed foreign to her. She pointed at the chair by the bed. "Sit. How may I help you?"

He sat and shifted in the chair a few times before settling down. "I know you're keeping secrets," he finally said in a low voice, his eyes on his clasped hands. "I have no right to ask you for anything, but I have a question."

Eala looked at him with curiosity. "A question? About what?" He hesitated. "If it's about your brother…"

He lifted his eyes and a hand to her. "No, it's not about him," he rushed to explain. "It's about your tattoo."

With a tilt of her head, Eala knitted her brows. "What about it?" Had he made the connection? It was such an outrageous one that she was willing to bet he didn't, but Cathal was not your ordinary man with pedestrian, unimaginative ideas.

A loud sigh escaped his mouth, and she found herself transfixed by the fullness of his lips as he bit down on them, gathering courage. "I saw that tattoo before," he said, gaze solidly on her eyes. "On one of your swans." Her heart skipped a beat. "How are you connected to the swans, Eala? Why are you and your people on this island, and why have we never heard of you? I mean, you're a queen; you'd think someone would know about you."

Was it time for the truth? Could she trust him that much to tell him the one thing only her people and the king knew about? Could she bear the shame?

"Like the swans, we are servants of the king," she said, opting for the half-truth instead. "We're kept on this island as a reward for our services." The word reward stuck on her throat, sour and acidic. Reward indeed; punishment was more like it. They were nothing more than glorified prisoners.

Something akin to panic stroked Cathal's handsome features. "So, it's true what they say about the swans and the king?" She tilted her head to better study him. Why did he seem agitated? His Adam's apple bobbed in his throat, and despite herself, Eala felt a frisson of yearning run through her. "You know, about the swan's—em, the swa-wan's kiss?"

Every ounce of warmth left Eala's body. How had he heard about that? The king kept it strictly under wraps so as not to invite others' envy and greed. "What do you mean?" she asked, voice trembling.

Cathal slumped on the chair, elbows braced on his legs and head almost touching his knees. "That a swan's kiss can keep you young and healthy?" Her stomach clenched, and a wave of nausea rippled through her. Holy Guardians, he knew! Was he putting the tattoo and the rumor together and coming out with the right guess? "Is the king having—I mean, is he—" Cathal stumbled over his words, his face a sickly hue of green. He paused for a moment, took a deep breath, and raised his eyes to hers. "Is he sleeping with the swans?"

Eala was not sure whether to laugh or cry. There

was truth in what he said, just not the way he thought. The king was a degenerate greedy man who stopped at nothing to reach his goals, and one of his main goals was to live longer than anyone else and rule the kingdom with an iron fist. She wouldn't put it past him to consider being intimate with a bird if it meant saving his hide, but that was not what was happening.

She chose to laugh, a tremulous hesitant soft chuckle that sounded fake even to herself. "No, it's not like that at all," she said, choking on her own words. It was so much worse, but she wasn't ready to tell him yet. "No bestiality involved." Half-truths were easier than full ones.

A faint smile stretched on Cathal's lips. "Oh, thank the Guardians for that," he breathed out. There was such a greenish tint to his skin still that she threw the sheets away and sat on the edge of the bed before him. "I'm a bit nauseous," he said, wrapping his arms around his middle.

She jumped to her feet and ran to fetch a pail, barely making it back before he emptied his stomach. He held the bucket between his hands while she rubbed a hand over his back. "I will make you some ginger tea." She stood up and padded on bare feet to her tea station, a small marble top table by the wall where a pretty ceramic kettle and an array of cups and saucers were kept. "Take deep breaths, in and out," she instructed while she poured tea into one of the cups and stirred some honey into it.

After sipping the tea, Cathal progressively got better, color returning to his cheeks as the heaves became less and less frequent. "I'm sorry, Eala," he said, wiping his lips with the cloth she had given him. "I don't know what came over me."

Eala poured herself some tea and sat on the edge of the bed. "How come the rumor got you that upset?" she asked, leaning over her knees. "I mean, I understand that the idea is enough to make anyone sick, but you're not related to the king and don't seem to particularly think much of him…" She left it hanging, not wanting to push so far that he'd shut her out.

"I thought—" He hesitated, stealing a glance at her. "I rescued one of your swans ten years ago." The breath caught in her throat, but she made herself look calm. "I became very attached to it because the creature seemed to understand what I said." He snorted. "I told the swan things I had never told anyone, and I felt as if it listened to me, as if it encouraged me to speak." He was silent for a while, lost in thought. "Anyway, the thought that the swan was being abused by King Rian made me sick to my stomach."

Eala closed her eyes and sighed. What would he think if he knew the truth? The truth that was much worse than what he'd imagined? Would he still look up to her? Or would he simply despise her much like she despised herself?

Eala watched Cathal leave her quarters, a little wobbly after vomiting his insides. The temptation to ask him to stay with her had been so strong, she had drawn blood on her lip to stop herself. But in the end, he had insisted on going to his own room, afraid of what the others would think if he lingered in hers for too long. She didn't bother to tell him the others would probably be happy that she had some honest and wholesome company; they knew the sacrifices she had made to keep them safe and sound.

Fearful he might collapse on the way, she followed him, hiding in the shadows of a full moon night. Much to her surprise, he veered off the path to his quarters and headed down the hill toward the lake. Funny how he seemed attracted by water as if it sang to him like a siren's song. She had met him first on the beach, and here on the island, she followed him to the lake every day. Her heart nearly exploded with a joy she hadn't known in years, watching him dip his feet in the water, splashing it on young Padraig, who squealed in delight. Cathal's laughter was a balm for her aching soul.

Cathal walked slowly all the way down the hill to where it flattened and leveled. He stood still, staring at the glittering waters for a while before dropping to his knees and slumping almost to the ground. His curved back shook, and Eala realized with a jolt that he was crying. An overwhelming sadness replaced the earlier lightness in her chest. She hesitated for a moment, and then, making a decision, she stepped into the open from behind the trees where she'd been hiding and rushed to his side.

She crouched beside him, studying him, not sure of what to do. "Cathal, are you all right?" she whispered, not wanting to startle him. He turned his head to glance at her; tears streamed down his cheeks from red-rimmed eyes. With a gasp, he looked away from her and covered his face with his hands. The last thing she wanted was for him to feel embarrassed. "I'm here, Cathal. I'm here for you. No need to hide. I know you're hurting."

At first, he didn't do anything, his sobs silenced by the palm of his hand, but then his shoulders dropped, and he leaned against her, placing his head on the flat of her shoulder, and cried. A bit taken aback by his reaction, Eala soon got on her knees and wrapped her arms around him, bringing him closer to her.

"I'm here," she repeated. And she meant it.

The moon bathed them and everything around them with its soft milky glow while the silence of the night lulled them into a soothing sense of peace. Eventually, Cathal's quiet sobs subsided, but he made no move to pull away from her. Instead, he leaned in closer, his hand resting on one of her arms, warm and inviting. She didn't want to move. It was heavenly having him in her arms, his ear close to her heart. She was certain he could hear it pounding. Eala chided herself for her foolishness. When had she became a silly girl so infatuated with a man, she couldn't think of anything else? There was no room for love in her life, a life that belonged to the king, not herself.

She made as to push him away, but he held onto her. "Don't," he said, his words muffled by her dress. "Stay, please."

Cathal raised his head to stare at her, eyes still red and wet, and she couldn't help but wish things were different, that she was someone else, someone who could indulge in loving this beautiful and kind man. But she was Eala, Queen of the Swans and Saintess. Healing powers coursed through her veins, a power that invited greed. A power that ultimately had changed her life forever.

"Why?" she asked. "Why do you cry?"

His smile was timid. "Life, I guess," he said, a tiny chuckle punctuating his words. "Why does life have to be difficult and unfair? I feel crushed by my responsibilities—and guilty for feeling that way." He lowered his face back to her shoulder. "My brother, my mother, Mhamó, even the swan I rescued from my brother's hands…why can't things be happier, lighter?"

Of all people, Eala had no answer to that question. She herself was a victim of unscrupulous individuals and her own bad choices. There was no way out in sight for her—not if she wanted to continue to protect her siblings.

She gently squeezed his shoulder, her other hand brushing over his thick hair. "You'll soon be free of one burden," she said, knowing all too well that loss would be another weight in his conscience. "I understand he's your brother and that you naturally want to protect him, but he's a monster, Cathal. Why can't you see that?"

Cathal was quiet for a bit, so still that, for a moment, she thought he had fallen asleep. When he spoke, his voice carried the agony of someone stuck between two impossible choices, "I do see it. I know the world would be a better, safer place without him, but my mother was adamant about protecting him. And I can't renege on an oath made to a dying woman, can I?"

Eala was mystified by that promise, not that he had made it, but why his mother had been insistent he did. His brother had obviously always been a burden for the family, and even a mother's heart would have realized it was not fair to sacrifice a good, kind child for a cruel one. There had to be more to the story, something Cathal was not aware of. She'd make some inquiries when she next visited the king. Her stomach lurched at the thought; that time was coming up way too fast.

"Eala?" The whisper took her by surprise. She pulled away enough to see the plea in his eyes. "I'm tired, so very tired."

She closed her eyes and inhaled deeply. "I know," she said with a long exhale. She was tired too—emotionally drained.

After a moment, he shuffled and lowered his head to her lap. Startled at first, she soon gave in to the pleasant feeling of human warmth and stretched on the cool grass, Cathal's head still cushioned by her thighs. She looked at the full moon in the sky, and she could have sworn it winked at her. Eala's eyes grew heavy with sleep, and she didn't fight it. For the first time in months, slumber came to her quickly and easily.

CHAPTER NINE
The Kiss

Cathal

The tantalizing scent of food wafted to his nose, and he took a deep breath, enjoying every minute of it. Cathal stirred the flakes of grilled fish into the steamed rice, sprinkled it with chopped green onions, added a few drops of sesame oil, and took a sniff. It smelled heavenly. He scooped some of the rice mixture into his hand and began working it into small rice balls. Growing up without much, his mom had taught him early on how to make mouthwatering food with scraps.

"Can I taste it?" Padraig could barely disguise his excitement and rocked on the balls of his feet, stretching his neck over Cathal's shoulders to take a peek at the food.

Cathal smiled. The boy, barely sixteen, had the appetite of a wolf, always too happy to help him with the leftovers of the lavish meals Eala and her people served him several times a day.

He turned around and handed him one of the rice balls, nestled in a pale cream paper cup. "Here, tell me what you think."

The boy scarfed down the food, his eyes widening to full circles. "This is so good," he said, bits of food flying out of his mouth with his words. Cathal laughed. "Sorry." Padraig wiped his mouth with the back of his hand and giggled, pink staining his cheeks. "The queen will love it."

Ever since being given the job of cleaning the kitchen, Cathal had been dying to cook a meal for Eala, but the royal cooks were not too open to the idea until Eala herself ordered them to let him do it. Cleaning was fine; he had always done a good job at it, but he longed to make Eala smile again like she had that day at the lake over a week ago. The food he cooked had often brought a smile to his mother's face; therefore, he couldn't wait to try it on the beautiful woman who had saved his life.

Cathal finished rolling the rice and placing the small savory bites in their paper cases, arranged it on the long oval serving dishes, surrounded by blooms gathered in the garden by Padraig, and wiped his hands to a towel, surveying his handiwork. "Ready," he announced with a satisfied grin.

Padraig didn't have to be told twice; he stepped forward and grabbed a couple of the dishes while

Cathal picked up a tray laden with the flower wine Eala's people brewed on the island. They stared at each other briefly and exchanged a conspiratorial nod before leaving the kitchen.

The queen and her other ten siblings, including the cooks, were all sitting at the long marble-top table in her quarters. Laoise and some of the others had set it up with beautiful glass stemless goblets and matching bowls. The chatter died down, and every eye turned to Cathal and his helper as they walked into the room. Eala gifted them with a smile that filled Cathal with a joy he was not used to.

The two men placed the trays on the table in silence. The food didn't look like much, but Cathal hoped it tasted as good as it smelled. There was a communal intake of air as the aroma hit everyone's noses.

Cathal pointed at one of the dishes. "Please, my Queen, help yourself," he said, a fist of anxiety tight around his heart. "I hope it meets with your approval."

Eala smiled again and stretched across the table to slide a couple of the rice balls into her bowl. "They look and smell delicious, Cathal," she said, the small praise growing wings inside him. Daintily, she popped one in her mouth and chewed it, closing her eyes for a moment and then swallowing. A new smile stretched her lips. "This is amazing, Cathal. So, so good." Cathal could fly if he tried. She turned to the others. "See for yourselves," she said, sweeping a hand in the air over the dishes. "Go on."

It was the green light they were all waiting for. All eleven of them, including Padraig, who had sat himself down across from Eala, descended on the dishes. Cathal sat on the chair next to the queen and watched them eat, a satisfied smile on his face.

"This is delicious," one of the females said, raising her goblet to him. "Well done, Cathal." The others all raised their glasses to him too with sounds of approval.

It was not so much that they liked his food, but it was the feeling they had accepted him in their midst that made him all warm and fuzzy inside. The suspicious glares and under-breath mutterings of the first few weeks had been replaced by grins and words of encouragement. He felt as if he belonged, as if he was part of their family now. He missed Mhamó and wished he could bring her to the island, but he couldn't deny the warmth in his heart and soul every time any of Eala's siblings smiled at him.

"Eat, Cathal," Eala said, sliding a rice ball into his bowl. Then, she added for his ears only, "Well done. Thank you."

If he smiled any wider, he'd pop the skin around his lips.

After lunch, Cathal waited for the others to disperse and began cleaning. Padraig joined him as he always did despite Cathal's protests. "This is my job, not yours."

The young man grinned and said, "My job is to take care of you, so, of course, helping you clean is part of my job."

Eala stood up and began collecting some of the dirty dishes. Cathal stopped her, placing his hand on her wrist. "You shouldn't do this. You're the queen. What are they going to think?"

She chuckled. "They will think that I'm helping clear the table. It's not the first time, you know." She looked pointedly at his hand, and he let her go. "I enjoy being busy, Cathal."

If anyone ever told him he would be washing dishes and sweeping floors alongside a queen, he would have laughed and called them crazy, but there he was doing just that. Eala wrapped a kitchen towel around her waist and took charge of the dishwashing while Cathal towel-dried the dishes, and Padraig swept and sang in a soft melodious voice.

It was the happiest he had ever been since his mother had died, and his stubborn grin refused to fade away. He was so intent on Padraig's song and Eala's sudsy hands, he would have missed the shadow across the window if it weren't for her cry of alarm. "Padraig, get him!"

Swift as the wind, the young man dropped the broom and flew out of the door in pursuit of who or whatever had been spying on them from outside. He glanced at Eala, worried. Who could possibly be? The gates had closed, and unless you were one of the swans or maybe the king, there was no way onto the island. The peace of a moment ago shattered. They both wiped their hands and exchanged confused looks.

Padraig soon returned, holding another young man by the collar. Despite the sword that hung from the intruder's belt, Padraig had the upper hand. "Here he is, my Queen. What shall I do with him?"

Eala sighed, her eyes hard as icicles. "You are not allowed on this side of the island," she said in a dangerously low tone. "Should I report this to the king?"

The young man blanched. "No, please don't," he pleaded, trying to drop to his knees, but Padraig wouldn't let him go. "I was only curious."

She studied him for a moment, sweat beading on the young man's forehead. "What's your name?"

"Lee, my name is Lee," the man said. "Please, have mercy."

"Are you new?"

Lee nodded. Cathal wondered what she meant by that. Was he one of the guards she sometimes mentioned? He had never seen them anywhere on the island, but then again, he hadn't ventured far from his quarters.

"You know what will happen if the king knows you've strayed to our side of the island, don't you?" The loud gulp was answer enough. "I suggest you keep what you saw to yourself, and I will pretend I didn't see you either, understand?" The young man nodded again. Eala turned to Padraig. "Tell Laoise to give him some tea before he goes back."

Cathal knitted his brows together. Tea? Why would she offer tea to someone who had obviously broken the rules?

Padraig pulled on the man's collar and pushed him forward. "Let's go." Lee muttered a thank you and stumbled out of the kitchen, half-hanging from Padraig's hold. Cathal watched them go, questions percolating inside his head.

"You're wondering about the tea, aren't you?" Eala asked, resuming her dishwashing as if nothing had happened. He nodded, too stunned to speak. "It's a special herbal tea. It will put him to sleep for a few hours, and when he wakes up, he will have only a vague memory of what he saw. In fact, he will believe he dreamed it all."

"Why don't you want him to report on what he saw?" he asked, finding his voice. "We weren't doing anything wrong."

She rubbed the soapy cloth in circles on the dish she was holding, her eyes never leaving it. "Because Cathal, the only reason you and your brother are still alive is because the king doesn't know you're here."

Cold flooded Cathal's being. Of course, how could he have forgotten? He was but a trespasser on the island, a crime punishable by death.

THE time they spent together was kept in Cathal's heart and memory as a treasure that could never be replaced. He would have never imagined he could feel that happy, that satisfied with life. He knew his status on the island was precarious at best, but he couldn't be bothered to think too much about it. Even the fact his brother was a prisoner, which ironically kept Odhran safe and sound for the moment, allowed Cathal to breathe easier for a change.

Eala joined him almost daily at the lake for a swim, and his wonder for the beauty of his surroundings was quickly replaced by the awe he couldn't hide every time he laid eyes on her. When she climbed out of the lake, her shoulder-length hair dripping water over her flawless freckled face, crystal droplets stuck to her eyelashes, and her white undergarments clinging to her body, it was all he could do not to melt like a caramel out in the sun for too long. In the past couple weeks, the gratitude he felt for her had grown into something much stronger, much more permanent and mightier; a feeling so powerful, he had trouble not touching her, not drawing her into his arms and—and what? This was a queen, a woman protected by a cruel king who wouldn't hesitate to chop off his head should he dare to lay a finger on her. A woman who was so far above him, fate had to have made a mistake bringing them together even for a moment.

"A coin for your thoughts." Eala was sitting on the grass less than an arm's length from him, squeezing water from her hair, her head tilted, and eyes glittering in amusement.

He raised his gaze to hers, that now familiar pang in his chest making him gasp at her beauty. She took his breath away. "I'm just happy," he admitted, his eyes refusing to stop studying her; her flaming hair, her unusual blue-green eyes, her ivory skin speckled here and there with light brown freckles like a robin's egg. "It seems wrong somehow."

Her hand stopped mid-way through her hair twist, her smile faded. "Why wrong? Are you not allowed a moment of happiness?"

Embarrassed by his admission, Cathal chuckled nervously. "With my brother in prison and Mhamó all alone in Nem, I can't help but feel guilty," he said, wiping his hands on his wet pants. "Also, I can't help but feel I am putting you and the others in danger. I mean, it's a criminal act for me to be here. What would happen to you if the king found out?"

Eala didn't flinch. "He won't find out," she said, such authority in her tone that Cathal couldn't doubt her. "As long as you keep to this side of the island and don't wander off to the other side where the guards live, they will never know."

It was out before he had the chance to think about it. "What if one of the others tells them?"

If a moment ago she hadn't seemed concerned about his comments, her forehead creased into a frown. "My siblings would never do that," she said, a rumble behind each word. "Betraying any of us would be the end of them. Their lives depend on keeping your brother's and your existence a secret."

Had she inadvertently revealed something she would rather not? Her bright eyes hid behind her light lashes, and her lips stretched into a tight line. Before he could stop it, he raised his hand and brushed it across her cheek. At first, she flinched, but seconds later, she leaned into his touch. He swallowed hard, electricity lighting up every cell on his body, a surge of such yearning like he had never experienced before.

He angled his face closer to hers, his eyes never drifting from her lips, red and plump like cherries in the summer. Would they be just as sweet? She glanced up then, her gaze a mixture of sorrow and joy, and he hesitated for a moment, his fingers still touching her face, trailing a fluttery path from her ear to her mouth. He waited, not sure his advances were welcomed. But when she smiled, a tremulous movement of her chin, a slow parting of her lips, Cathal crossed the remaining space between them and kissed her—a butterfly touch of the lips at first. Eala touched his face in a barely-there caress that set him on fire. His kiss deepened, his tongue stroking hers, her taste—sweet as he expected—mingling with his. He could linger in that moment forever and be perfectly content.

"My Queen." Padraig's voice broke the spell of their moment, and they pulled away from each other as if stung by a bee. The young man came around the bend on the path, carrying a note in his hands. Cathal wondered whether he had witnessed the kiss, but by the casual expression on his face, he guessed not. "A message came for you."

Cathal couldn't deny his admiration—and a little disappointment—at Eala's cool and collected reaction to the boy's interruption. It was as if they hadn't been physically connected a moment ago. She turned her upper body toward Padraig and smiled, her lips swollen and wet. "What is it, Padraig?"

The young man bent down and handed her the note. "It came from Nem," he said. Cathal could have sworn Eala's face blanched as she quickly opened and began reading it. "How's the water?" the boy asked Cathal with a grin. He often joined them for a swim, but he had been deployed somewhere else on the island today.

"Nice and cool as usual," Cathal replied. "You should have joined us."

"Mail day," the boy said simply, throwing a curious glance at his queen, whose color had returned to her cheeks. "Any news?"

Eala, her usual coolness restored, smiled at him and then looked at Cathal. "Yes, great news for our guest," she said. Cathal raised his eyebrows. "This is a message from Lily Pad. She's coming back tomorrow and bringing your grandmother with her."

THAT kiss by the lake was not mentioned again, and Cathal couldn't deny a certain bitterness; he'd hope Eala would want to talk about it. It was not as if they had done it before, and it held so much promise—from her, from him—it seemed anti-climactic and certainly disappointing that she seemed to have forgotten about it.

That conversation would have to wait. He paced in front of his quarters, waiting for news about Mhamó. She was due to arrive sometime that afternoon, but the site or even how she'd arrive was being kept under wraps. The gate was closed, so how would they get his grandmother through? Questions for another day too. All he wanted at that moment was to set his eyes on Mhamó.

"Are you just going to stand there, or do you want to see your grandmother?" Eala appeared out of nowhere, a small knowing smile on her lips. "We have settled her in her new quarters down the path. Want to come see her?"

Cathal knew she was teasing him, but he played along anyway. "What do you think? Of course, I want to see her. I thought you were bringing her here."

Eala took a few steps toward him and offered him her hand. "She's an old woman, and she was tired," she said. "I thought it would be better if you went to see her instead."

He stared at her outstretched hand, pondering the wisdom of taking it; a simple touch of her skin was

enough to burn him to a crisp. In the end, he risked it. "You did the right thing," he whispered, the warmth of her palm quickly spreading to every inch of him. "Let's go."

She led him around the building and down the back path for a few minutes to a small structure that was a miniature version of the others. "I figured she'd be more comfortable in a small place. Less walking, less cleaning."

Cathal's smile spread from ear to ear. "Thank you."

Eala dropped his hand. "Go. No one will disturb you." When he hesitated, she pointed forward with her chin. "Go! I will send someone with food in a bit."

Mhamó was sitting on a chair by one of the open windows and didn't see him when he walked in. He watched her for a moment. She had aged in the couple months they'd been parted, her hair whiter, if that was even possible, her time-worn face thin and haggard. Guilt gnawed at his heart. He'd been here all that time, being cared for and pampered while his grandmother worried and faded away.

"Mhamó," he called, crossing the space between them. She didn't hear him; thus, he called again, louder this time, "Mhamó!"

She turned to him, her haunted brown eyes softening and filling with joy. She chuckled and rose from the chair. "My sweet Cathal," she said, opening her arms to him. "I missed you."

Wrapping his long arms around the small body of

his grandmother, Cathal suppressed a sob—of joy or sadness, he couldn't be sure. "Mhamó, you're here. I'm so happy to see you."

Those hands that had often comforted him to sleep or treated his injuries now flattened on his back, weak but warm, familiar. "You're looking good, *garmhac*," she said, her voice as strong as he remembered. "Have the swan people been treating you well?"

He nodded and pulled away to stare at her. She had always been tiny like his mother, but with age, she seemed to shrink even more, her head barely reaching his chest height. "They have been wonderful, Mhamó. Has Lily Pad treated you nicely?"

Grandma chortled and waved a hand. "That wisp of a girl? Such a hard worker for such a young thing." He smiled and pointed to the chair. She sat down. "I don't know where she's gone, but you need to meet her." He couldn't wait to thank her, but for now, he was glad it was just the two of them. Her laughter faded. "Where's your brother? Is he alive?"

Cathal nodded and pulled a chair close to hers. "The queen has kept him alive for now," he explained, taking a seat. "But he hurt the sacred swans. The king will want him dead."

Mhamó snorted. "Don't be so sure." What did she mean by that? "The king is a cruel man with lots of secrets."

"So does our family," he heard himself say. Why was he bringing this up now? Grandma had just arrived, and there he was, already bringing up the secrets that had haunted him since childhood. "Why must we protect Odhran? He's evil. He has no love for anyone besides himself and shows no remorse for any of the bad things he's done."

The old woman sighed deeply. "One day, *garmhac*. One day, I will tell you, but for now, let me look at you." She made a big production of studying him. "You've grown handsome these past months. You're a man now." He laughed. He'd been a man long before coming of age. He had had no choice but to grow up quickly. "Is there any food in this place? I'm a bit peckish."

As if on cue, Laoise and a younger woman he didn't recognize walked in with trays laden with food and drink. "Our queen sent us with these," Laoise said with her usual aloofness. "Put it down on that table, Lily Pad."

Lily Pad was about the same height and age as Padraig, with chubby cheeks and twinkling dark eyes. "I brought you those pastries you like, Granny," she said with a generous smile.

"Cathal, this is my girl, Lily Pad," the old woman said, pleasure thickening her voice. "You can call her sister because I decided to adopt her."

Lily Pad laughed and set the tray down on a table. "Hello, brother, glad to finally meet you." She straightened and curtsied. She had the friendliest face he had ever seen, not necessarily pretty but attractive in her pleasant manners. She leaned over a bit and pretended to whisper to him, "I'm also glad that I have someone to share her care with now. She can be difficult."

Instead of being angry, his grandmother let out a whole-hearted laugh. "Cheeky girl! I will tan your hide."

Cathal had never heard his grandmother be this playful. Back in Nem, life was hard and gloomy, and there were not a lot of reasons to laugh. It was heartwarming that the young woman had managed to change that.

"You love me too much, Granny," Lily Pad quipped and handed his grandma one of the pastries. "Here, you haven't eaten in hours."

Laoise was quiet as usual, but Cathal was shocked to catch the tiniest of smiles kicking the corners of her lips as she stood to a corner, watching the lively exchange. "All right, young woman," she said after clearing her throat. "It's time for you to go report to the queen and for Mrs. Ó Broin to rest."

Cathal was startled by the mention of their family name. He couldn't remember when he last had heard it, but of course, others wouldn't call his grandmother Mhamó; she had a name. He tried hard to recall it, but he couldn't remember. The most common of things, such as a name, had long been lost for him when the struggle to survive took all his energy.

"Call me Cara, dearie," Mhamó said, a youthful

smile on her face. "No one has called my name in over twenty years. It will be nice to hear it again."

Cathal's heart shattered; he had not been the only one in his family who had sacrificed it all to protect first his mother and then his cruel brother.

"Well, Cara," Laoise said, the warmth in her voice strange to Cathal's ears. "You catch up with your grandson and rest. The queen will come to welcome you later."

His eyes bounced from the usually cold woman to his grandmother's face; she seemed younger somehow from only moments ago as if being there and knowing the world was safe from Odhran, for now, was all she needed to breathe again.

CHAPTER TEN

Cara

Eala

The arrival of Cathal's grandmother was a welcomed distraction from her thoughts. Eala hadn't had the time to think about that kiss by the lake. She hadn't had the chance to ponder on its meaning and, more pressing, its consequences. She knew better than to fall for anyone; she knew a lover was not in her cards. Because of who she was—*what* she was— she'd never be allowed the privilege of a love life. As a Saintess, she couldn't afford to be selfish and indulge in a relationship that could not go anywhere; her people's safety and future depended on her. But she had to admit, however reluctantly, that Cathal had stolen her heart. In fact, her heart, or what she had left of it, had been his for many years. She couldn't tell him because doing so would be revealing the secret that kept her siblings alive while also keeping them captive.

As she walked across the settlement to where the old woman was housed, her hands and legs felt jittery, as if charged with static electricity. Cathal would be there, and she knew the memory of his soft lips would come flooding back to her. And so would the harder memories of what she had done that had caused her people to lose their freedom.

"Are you coming in or are you going to stand there staring into empty space?" Laoise stood in the doorway with an amused twist on her lips and her hands primly clasped in front of her. "Master Cathal has been eagerly waiting for you."

For a brief moment, Eala was carried back to when she was a young girl being teased by her older sister, and she rolled her eyes. "I'm not staring," she felt the need to clarify, "I'm thinking."

The older woman snorted. "Right. You forget, my Queen, that I have known you for almost twenty-nine years." Her eyes softened. "You're allowed to love, Eala. You deserve to be loved."

Eala lowered her eyes and smoothed imaginary wrinkles from her dress. "You know as well as I do that I can't." It was merely a whisper, but it carried the weight of the world. "I messed up, and now, I'm paying for my mistake."

Laoise dropped her cool demeanor and stepped closer to her queen, reaching out for her hands. "Don't give up so easily," she said, urgency in her tone. "We'll find a way around it, you'll see. This won't be forever."

The queen swallowed the giant knot in her throat along with the tears that burned in her eyes. "I'm resigned to my fate," she whispered, relishing the heat of her sister's hand. "Don't you worry about me, sister."

Cathal was fussing over his grandmother, trying to coax her into eating more. Eala stopped for a second, watching their exchange of words and body language, the old woman swatting her grandson's hands away, pretending to be annoyed by his insistence, and Cathal's stubbornness prevailing.

As soon as Mhamó spotted Eala, she waved her closer. "Dearie, can you please use your royal authority to tell him to stop badgering me about food?" she said, a feigned expression of annoyance on her wrinkled face. "I'm an old woman. I can't eat like a young one, right? Can you take him away so I can have some peace?"

Eala hid a chuckle with her fist, cleared her throat, and said, "Cathal, will you leave your grandmother alone, please? Laoise could use your help in the kitchen." Laoise bristled at this suggestion, a few inarticulate sounds escaping her lips. "Let me talk with Mrs. Ó Broin in private."

The old woman caught her eye and grinned—not the smile of a tired old woman, but that of a mischievous girl who just got her way. "Yes, *garmhac*, go do some work. Idle hands are the devil's workshop," she said, shooing him away with her hands. "I'd love to have a chat with this lovely woman."

Cathal's face fell as he threw a pleading glance at Eala. She hid another chuckle. "Go, Cathal." She turned to Laoise, whose face had turned a light shade of red. "Sister, give him something to do in the kitchen, and don't let him out of your sight until I say."

Her words left no margin for discussion, so Laoise, still flustered by the order, escorted a confused Cathal out of the room. Eala crossed over to where the old woman was sitting and pulled another chair for herself. When she raised her eyes, she was surprised to find Cara's brown gaze on her. Eala smiled.

"Well, Mrs. Ó Broin, what exactly do you need to talk to me about?" Eala asked in a soft voice that belied her curiosity. "You just met me for the first time, and yet, I get the feeling you know me. Why is that?"

Cathal's grandma clicked her tongue. "I never actually met you, but I know who you are," she said, pointing a gnarled finger at her. "Ten years ago, my grandson saved you from his lunatic brother." Eala's heart must have stopped for a second because she couldn't breathe. "Yes, Eala, I know you're one of the sacred swans."

For the first time in years, Eala caught herself gawking, mouth half-open and eyes that felt as if they would explode out of their sockets. How did this woman know her secret when even Cathal hadn't put it together yet? "H-h-how?" she stuttered, her usual cool leaving her completely.

Ó Broin reached across the small table that separated them and patted her hand. "My grandson is a lovely man with the kindest heart one can wish for," she said. "But he's so busy surviving and protecting his brother and me that he misses things. I'm old and like to pretend I can't hear very well because then I am privy to information I wouldn't otherwise have access to."

Eala had to give the woman credit; she was a cunning creature. She liked this old woman. "How did you find out about us? Cathal doesn't know."

"My poor *garmhac* is too focused on his responsibilities, and sometimes, he doesn't see what's right in front of him," the old woman said with a click of her tongue. "I overheard a conversation between him and Odhran about the swan, so that night, when he thought I was asleep, I followed him to the *scioból*." It still didn't explain how she knew Eala was one of the sacred swans Odhran was determined to hunt. Ó Broin seemed to read her mind. "When you've been around for as long as I have been and seen all that I have seen, it's not hard to put two and two together. When your lovely Lily Pad came to take care of me, the pieces began to fall into the right place, and when she brought me here, I had no doubt left in my mind. Who else could have brought me to Swan Island while the gates were closed?"

What could she say after that? Deny it? There wasn't much point, was it? "I hope you'll agree to keep it a secret," she finally said. "All of our lives depend on it."

"I will keep your secret if you keep mine." What the old woman told her next blew her away. It looked as if Eala was not the only one keeping secrets.

EALA was still reeling from the information Cathal's grandmother had shared with her. What this meant to her and her people, she couldn't be sure, but a small flame of hope from deep inside her flared. She left the old woman in the capable care of young Lily Pad and went in search of Cathal, her mind working overtime, trying to come up with an excuse for what she was about to do.

The warmth and heavenly scents of the kitchen hit her as she crossed the doorway. Cathal was stirring a large pot, his face over the thick white steam, his forehead furrowed in concentration. She paused for a moment and watched him, a smile tugging at her lips. Everything Cathal did was masterful; he didn't do anything in halves, instead putting all he had into it, no matter if it was sweeping the courtyard or coming up with an exquisite meal. She was willing to guess he would put an equally enthusiastic effort into learning how to fight. Her siblings could help him with that.

They were a race of healers, but one who wouldn't be defenseless in case of an attack. *Not that our fighting skills did any of us any good against the king*, she thought with a sigh. What could twelve of them do, no matter how talented they were, fighting against an army of thousands? Instead, they hid the fact they were all trained in man-to-man combat. It was wise not to divulge too much to the enemy; her master had taught her that. Her stomach clenched at the memory of the woman who had been more than a teacher to her, who had loved her and protected her until—

The memory was too painful.

She shook her thoughts away and walked into the kitchen. "Guardians be blessed, what's this I smell?" she exclaimed, her cheerful tone belying the ache in her heart.

Cathal raised his eyes to her and smiled, the skin around them crinkling like silk paper. He was beautiful. "Eala, you're here. Come!" He beckoned her with a hand. "This is my grandmother's favorite dumpling soup. Come taste it and tell me what you think."

Eala inhaled the delicious smells of the kitchen and sidled beside him by the large pot over the fire. He scooped a spoonful of soup from inside and offered it to her after gently blowing on it. As soon as her lips closed around the spoon, she let out a moan. It was heavenly, like comfort in edible form.

"Well done, Cathal," she said as soon as she had swallowed the soft, tasty dumpling along with the flavorful hot broth. "Ó Broin will be impressed."

The satisfied stretch of his lips made her happy. This was a man who rarely got praised, if ever. She remembered the things he told her in that old building while she recovered from her grave injuries ten years ago, things he thought he was revealing to an animal who wouldn't judge or repeat it. He hadn't known then she was that swan, the creature his brother had shot through the shoulder, that inside the feathery body was a human heart. Every night, he would come with food, homemade medicine, and, best of all, human company. He'd lay down by her, his calloused hand caressing her wings and neck, his head often leaning against her, and he'd confide in her, telling her things she knew no one had ever heard from him; things he carried inside, emotional wounds to match the ones he had on his body. No one ever praised him even when he took the blame for his brother's trespasses or when he did whatever he needed to do to bring sustenance to his family. Even his grandmother, however proud she was of him, kept her thoughts to herself, perhaps thinking it would help build his defenses against a world that was anything but kind.

She cleared her throat, suddenly overwhelmed by an emotion she had long forbidden herself to feel. "After you eat, will you come to see me in my quarters?" By then, maybe she would have been able to come up with a believable reason for her actions. Ó Broin had made her promise not to reveal the real one and, considering what that might mean to her and her swans, she would comply.

Cathal tilted his head in such a bird-like fashion, she almost laughed. Maybe there was some swan inside him after all. "Of course," he said, his eyebrows knitted together. "Any problem?"

Her hands went up in front of her. "No, no problem. I just want to discuss something with you." The worried expression he gave her made her add, "Nothing bad, I swear. Should we say at nightfall?"

He nodded, and she turned around to leave. "I will have some of the soup sent to your quarters, my Queen." She was used to being called that, but somehow those words coming from him—whether he intended it or not—had a totally different meaning, one that melted her insides and brought a silly smile to her lips. She couldn't wait to see the joy and surprise in his eyes when she told him she'd be sparing his brother's life, after all.

CHAPTER ELEVEN

The Swan

Cathal

He stared at her, mouth half-opened, trying to process what Eala had told him. After stressing over the fate of his brother for weeks, Cathal could barely believe the queen had decided against executing Odhran or turning him in to the king's guards. He was torn between relief and worry—relieved for his brother but worried about what it might mean to Eala and her people.

"What if the king finds out you're harboring a criminal?" he asked her. "Aren't you risking too much?"

Eala chuckled, setting the teacup on the small round table between them. "I thought you'd be happy that I'm keeping your brother alive."

He opened and closed his mouth a couple times

before responding, "Yes, of course, I am. I'm eternally grateful, but I worry about you too. I don't want to put you or your people in any danger."

Laughter died on her lips, but her eyes softened further. "Thank you for caring, Cathal. It means a lot to me." The silkiness and warmth of her voice was as effective as a caress, and Cathal's body came alive. He had never felt such yearning, such need for another human being. "We can keep it under wraps for a while. That won't be a problem. The guards are not privy to our holding cells."

Even though he had no idea what had caused her sudden change of mind, he couldn't hold in the joy it brought. Cathal knew he looked like a child watching his first firework display. "Thank you, Eala," he whispered. "I owe you. Ask me anything, and I will do it."

Her youthful chortle made him smile. She couldn't be much older than he was but often seemed older with her serious, unsmiling demeanor. She had been smiling a lot more lately, and the results were breathtaking; not only did she look younger, but she appeared more beautiful if that was possible. He was mesmerized by her fiery wavy hair that reached just to her ivory shoulders, her unusual sparkling blue-green eyes that looked wise beyond her years, and the way freckles peppered the bridge of her nose and the top of her cheeks. Thin white fabric covered the rest of her, but he had seen her bare shoulders at the lake and the way her skin was stippled in a trail of light brown spots down to where her doudou hid them from sight. He had dreamed about what they looked like under the silky diamond of cloth, stretching across her chest and her breasts. He swallowed hard, his insides burning with the desire to follow that imaginary line with his fingers and lips.

"You look flushed," she said, and his cheeks burned even hotter. "Are you feeling sick?" She jumped to her feet, the skin between her well-shaped eyebrows furrowed, and placed a velvety hand on his forehead. "You do feel warm." Urgency tinted her voice now. "Come on, lie down for a bit."

It didn't matter that he knew all too well that his sudden rush of heat had nothing to do with his injuries or a fever; he obeyed, getting up and crossing the room to her bed, a simple but elegant wooden structure encased within a tent of diaphanous white cloth. Under her close scrutiny, he sat on the edge and watched her entranced while she removed his shoes and helped him stretch out on top of the light pastel coverings. Eala sat down at the bottom end of the bed, took one of his feet into her hands and began to gently but firmly massage it. Cathal was afraid to move, not sure what he would do if he allowed his body to do what it was begging him for. She was a queen, after all. How would she react to his advances? Someone as common as a garden weed, a man whose role in this world was minor at best and negligible at worst.

Her small hands stroked the soles of his feet, one at a time, her thumb pressing along the edges from his heel to his big toe and back again. It relaxed him as much as it stimulated him, fanning the fire inside. Eala proceeded to his legs, kneading his calves, his knees, and his upper thighs. Cathal uttered a silent prayer to the Guardians to keep him in control; the last thing he wanted to do was to offend the beautiful woman attending to him so generously.

When she deemed him relaxed—if only she knew how he felt—Eala stopped and bent down over him to check his forehead again, her touch rousing the pressure inside him and making him fearless. Before she could move away from him, he closed his hands around her waist and pulled her in.

She gasped, "What are you doing?" She braced her hands on either side of his head, her body awkwardly resting on his.

Breathing had become very hard for Cathal, but he managed to whisper, "Don't go, please."

Their eyes met, and for a moment, they said nothing, drinking each other in. Cathal hoped he hadn't offended her by his rash move, but if at first she had looked surprised, the wrinkles between her brows had eased away and her unfathomable eyes had grown warmer now. With a slight push, Eala rolled until they were lying side by side, facing each other.

"Can I kiss you?" Cathal asked, one of his hands still clasped on her waist. He was not sure how he'd react if she said no, but she nodded, and he didn't hesitate any longer. His lips closed on hers, electricity coursing throughout his body, melting all his defenses, erasing all his fears.

Eala parted her lips and allowed him in, welcoming his exploration with one of her own. Her flavor didn't disappoint, all sunshine and ocean air, a distant threat of a storm, one he was more than willing to face head-on. Beneath her mask of coolness, there was passion and fire.

With a moan, Cathal moved his lips to the length of her jaw and then down the side of her neck. He slid the fabric off her shoulder and kissed the smooth skin beneath. "You're beautiful, Eala," he whispered, peppering kisses all the way down her arm to the bend of her elbow and up again to her firm bicep. Something rough scratched his lips, and Cathal pulled away to see what it was. A small scar broke the smoothness of her skin, old, fully healed, and shaped like a tiny slit. Something clicked in his head, a memory, a fragment of a thought. Cathal turned her arm to look on the other side, and there it was, another scar. An exit wound, he realized with a jolt.

"You're—no, it can't be," he stuttered, his fingers touching the thin scar. "You can't be that swan." He looked up at her as if expecting her to deny it. She didn't. "How can this be? You're a human."

Eala closed her eyes for a moment. "I am one of the sacred swans, Cathal," she finally said, sadness shadowing her gaze. "I am the swan you saved ten years ago."

HOW was that possible? She was obviously a human, her soft body warm and exciting against his. How could Eala be the swan he had tended back to health all those years ago? Cathal's head swam, a million questions swirling around inside as he gazed into the sad eyes of the queen.

"All my people are swans," she said, licking her lips. "And human as well. We're the last of a sect of warrior healers who have served the great rulers of this world as well as anyone who ever needed our services."

The words were stuck in Cathal's throat. Was he dreaming? Maybe he was under the effects of a fever and was hallucinating. Eala brushed the side of her hand on his face. He shivered.

"We had lived in semi-seclusion for hundreds of years until about thirteen years ago when we were brought into King Rian's service and placed on this island permanently," she continued. Cathal wanted to erase the overwhelming sadness from her voice. "I am the Saintess, the queen of my swans, but I'm nothing more than a prisoner myself. That day at the beach was a terrible mistake, one that almost got us all killed."

He found his voice. "What do you mean by mistake?" All he wanted to do is draw her into his arms, kiss her again, and whisper sweet nothings in her ear. He didn't like the pain in her words, the torment in her gaze.

"I was young and foolish and thought I had more power than I really had," she explained with a sigh. "I thought the king would forgive me a small trespass. He used to give us a week every year to fly over the land in complete freedom. We were not to talk to anyone or show them our true forms, fly far from the coast. People could see us but not touch us, and at the end of the week, we were to go back to the island and stay for another full year." Her gaze was lost on some invisible horizon. "That beach looked empty. I told my swans they could fly close to land, maybe even swim in the waves. We didn't expect your brother to come chasing us."

Cathal cursed Odhran in silence. He remembered her bloody wing, the way her graceful head drooped over his arm as he carried her to the *scioból*. It still made him angry. "It was my fault. I was supposed to watch him, but he sneaked out of the house—"

Eala didn't let him finish, covering his lips with hers. The kiss tasted of anger and desperation. "Not your fault, Cathal," she said over his lips. "Nothing your brother has done is your fault."

Despite his wish to know more, to ask more questions, his need for her was stronger. He resumed the peeling off her dress, untying the straps that held it closed in the back, slipping it off her shoulder and down her arm, an extra log added to his fire with every inch of ivory skin revealed. He reached behind her graceful neck and undid the laces of her doudou, his heart racing so fast, he thought it might escape through bone and flesh. Without rushing, he pulled the silky diamond cloth from her, baring her small, perfect breasts.

A moan escaped his throat. He'd died a happy man right there and then. "You're perfect, my Queen," he whispered, covering one of her breasts with his hand. The smooth skin of her chest was lightly speckled as if someone had shaken cinnamon over it. It made his mouth water and his gut tighten. He glanced at her face seeking permission. Her eyes were semi-closed, her chin tilted up as she arched her back, surrendering to his caress. There was no further hesitation. Latching his lips around her breast, Cathal brushed his tongue over her velvety skin, lingering over her hardening nipple. Eala tasted as good as he had imagined.

With liquid fire running through his veins, Cathal moved his mouth down to her belly, kissing his way to the waist of her white pants. She whimpered when he squeezed his hand between the fabric and her hip, the green light he needed to pull down the garment, but she suddenly grabbed his hand. He arched his eyebrows, confused.

"Did I hurt you?" he asked, worried.

Eala sighed, her bare chest rising and falling with her breath. "No, of course not, Cathal. I want this, I do."

"Then why did you stop me?" he said, a bit breathless. "Did I make you uncomfortable?"

She shook her head, and he could swear there were tears in her eyes. "I can't, Cathal, I just can't."

"What do you mean?" A strange thought crossed his mind. "Is it because you're a swan? Is your anatomy different from a regular female?" It sounded stupid even to himself, but why else would she stop him from doing something she herself wished to do?

"I am as much of a woman as any other female, Cathal," she said, tear-choked. "That's not why."

Cathal wanted to press on but refrained from doing so. She needed time to collect herself, to decide whether to confide in him, and he would give her all the space and time she needed. He let go of her and sat up, his body still overheated and yearning for hers. Tears ran down her cheeks, and he couldn't stand seeing her upset. Grabbing the edges of the bed covers, he folded them over her, covering her naked chest.

"It's okay if you don't want to tell me," he said and meant it.

Eala pulled the covers closer to her chin and wiped her tears with the back of a trembling hand. "Do you know about the rumor, the one that claims a kiss from a sacred swan will not only cure you of any illness but prolong your life, make you younger?"

The conversation he had had with his brother a few weeks back came barreling back to him. Odhran had said that the king took a swan to his palace every month to serve him. Suddenly, it was hard to breathe. He nodded.

"It's not a rumor," Eala said, her eyes hidden behind her thick copper lashes. "It's a fact. Except for one detail. People think that any of the swans have that gift, but that's a myth. Only one swan can do it."

No, it couldn't be. It couldn't be.

"That swan is me." The dreaded words froze his blood. "The queen of the swan people is chosen because of that gift, not because of parentage or heritage. The gift manifests itself with the girl's first monthly cycle. The Saintess is then trained to use her gift, but it never, ever includes what I must do now to protect my people."

He was scared to ask. Deep inside, he knew what she was going to say, but he had to hear it from her. "What must you do to protect your swans?"

"When the king found out the rumor was real, he came to visit our settlement in the mountains." Eala's knuckles were white as she held on to the covers. "He wanted to know more about us, about this tribe of healers who could change into swans and fly. I was flattered by his attention, his promises… I swallowed it, hook, line, and sinker, dooming myself and my people to a life of servitude."

Cathal needed to touch her, to draw her into his

arms and comfort her, but he wasn't sure that was what she'd want at the moment. So, he stared helplessly, his hands fidgeting on his lap while she took another deep breath.

When she spoke again, her eyes were haunted by something he couldn't fathom. Her words nearly knocked him off the bed. "I might be a queen, Cathal, but I'm also the king's whore."

CHAPTER TWELVE

The King

How could she tell him the naked truth? The shame-drenched reality of her existence. In all these years since she had become the king's fountain of youth, she had never felt as ashamed as she did now, facing Cathal, the one man who had made her smile again, who made her want to fight for her freedom—a foolish desire, of course, when the lives of all her swans were on the table.

She had been barely seventeen when King Rian found her. The location of her settlements had always been kept in relative secret because her teacher, and all those before her, had been wise enough to realize that what the sacred swans could do would attract those with no scruples. But the king had found them nevertheless and had come to visit her. Aoibhe, her teacher and mentor, had passed away only a few months prior, and Eala was still grieving, overwhelmed by the new responsibilities suddenly thrown at her.

"No," she chided herself silently. There was no excuse for what she had done, no matter how young and inexperienced she was.

"He came at me with honey on his tongue and promises of protection for my people," Eala said to Cathal. She had put on her night robes, and they both sat around the table, across from each other. Cathal looked stricken as if someone had told him he had only a few hours to live. Her heart skipped a few beats, sorrow coursing through it. "I believed him—no, I wanted to believe him. I didn't want to shoulder the responsibility of taking care of my people alone. I was scared, devastated by the death of our queen, my master." She took a deep breath, hoping the oxygen would ease the weight on her chest. It didn't. "I was lonely, Cathal."

Cathal's hand twitched as if he was struggling not to reach across the table and touch her. "Why do you blame yourself, Eala?" It was a whisper. "You were young and overwhelmed. Put the fault where it should be. The king is the culprit here, not you."

It warmed her heart that he thought so, that he wasn't looking at her with the eyes of judgment. She couldn't bear that, not from him. "Aoibhe had taught me well. She told me not to trust those who made promises, those who praised you with sticky sweet words, those who made promises too good to be true. Yet, I did. I believed him."

She felt it before she saw it, Cathal's hand covering hers, his calloused thumb rubbing against her wrist. He offered her a hesitant smile. "You don't have to talk about it if you don't want to," he breathed, his eyes searching hers.

She shook her head, determined. "No, I do need to tell you. I've kept this inside for too long. My people know, and they don't judge me, but we've lived isolated from the rest of the world ever since. Therefore, I keep it all in, and it's killing me one cell at a time." She stared at their connected hands, relishing the comfort his warm palm provided. She continued, "The king brought me to his palace on numerous occasions. At first, it was thrilling. He treated me like a daughter, showering me with attention and showing me a world I barely knew existed. If I had been a little cautious in the beginning, I soon became careless, lulled by his appearance of fatherly kindness."

Cathal poured her some tea and pushed the cup in her direction. "It will soothe you a bit," he said. She took the cup and drank the tea in a big gulp, knowing all too well that nothing would ever soothe her about her circumstances.

She pressed on. "After a few months of spoiling me with what I thought was real affection, King Rian began changing the way he treated me. It was subtle at first, traces of something not right, something malicious beneath his graces. I dismissed it, thinking I was being ungrateful and overly suspicious. He had showered my people with gifts, and I was glad that for once, they were rewarded for all they did for others." She snorted. "Queen Aoibhe always taught me that the work of swan healers did not require a reward. That the honor of helping others was all the payment we ever needed. Stupidly, I wanted more for them—not me, I never wanted anything for me."

She hung her head, tears burning in her eyes. She did want something; she had wanted love. Eala had grown up without parents. The then-queen had cared for her like a mother, but Eala always felt that emptiness inside, a hole she did not know how to fill. King Rian's feigned care filled that space for a while, only to rip her apart later.

"One day, he invited me to his quarters for tea," she said, bile burning her throat. "It was not unusual for him to meet me in his room, and I had no reason to suspect anything amiss. I was so stupid, so naive." Cathal's hand came to rest on hers again, soothing. "He came clean then: I either accepted his terms, or he would kill my swans." She took yet another deep breath. "The terms were simple. I would have sex with him once a month to keep him young and healthy, and he would keep my swans protected."

Cathal's hand shook, and his breath caught. "Bastard, how can he be such a snake?"

Eala clenched her teeth hard enough to hurt. "He

also forbade us from caring for the sick. We were to cater only to him and the royal family." She knew he was still wondering why she couldn't make love to him when she so obviously wanted to. "This gift—curse, really—is not inexhaustible. I must recover my strength after each visit to the palace. If I was to consummate our relationship, Cathal, it would weaken its power, and the king would be able to tell. He wants to live forever, and if that means keeping me as his whore and not allowing any other male around me, that's what he'll do. That's why no one is allowed on the island, and even the guards are to be kept away from our settlement."

Cathal blanched, squeezing her hand harder. "You now have two uninvited males here," he exclaimed. "By the Guardians, if the king finds out, you'll be dead!"

The king would never kill her, not while she could make him young and vital, but he would kill one or two of her swans just to prove a point. She was tired though, so very tired of obeying him, of living in fear of what he might do. Eala was fed up with being told not to do what she had been born to do, sick of dreading the times she secretly sent one of her swans to help someone in need.

"I talked to my swans, and they begged me to let you stay," she confessed, fully aware that she wanted that too. "We'll just have to be careful."

What she didn't tell him, because Cathal's

grandmother had asked her not to, was that she was now in possession of something, an ace card that could potentially change their lives forever. It was risky, but it was more than she had ever had since the king, in his greed, had taken her into his bed.

CHAPTER THIRTEEN

Shattered

Cathal

There were exactly five hundred and fifty bamboo rectangles on Cathal's ceiling. He had spent most of the last hour counting them as he lay on his back, an arm behind his head and a mind so full of disturbing thoughts that the boring task of counting ceiling tiles had become a welcoming respite.

How could he process what Eala had revealed to him the day before? His emotions teetered between anger and sorrow. The need to comfort her fighting with the wish to storm into the palace and kill the king. He would never make it close enough to do that, but the mere thought, the fantasy of plunging a sword deep into the belly of the corrupt monarch, made him grin in morbid satisfaction. Cathal had never had any wish to kill anyone or anything until now.

"As long as King Rian wants me to keep him young and healthy, we can't be together, Cathal," Eala had told him in the wee hours of the night when they had lain side by side on the bed, unable to touch each other for fear of losing control and damning all the swans. "It takes exactly thirty days to replenish my healing energy. He would know."

Cathal didn't want to think about how the king would be able to tell her healing powers were not fully recharged. That would imply imagining the degenerate ruler entwined with the beautiful queen, on and inside her. He couldn't breathe when even a flicker of the thought escaped his careful attempts at focusing on boring, irrelevant things. One of the chairs and a ceramic teacup lay in pieces as witnesses to the times he had not been able to stop such images from intruding into his thoughts.

"Why am I such a nobody?" he yelled, punching the bed. "Why don't I have any power?"

He was nothing, less than nothing. He didn't even register in the infinity of the universe—an ant, only good to work and be squashed under someone's boots. He could hold his own in a fight but had no real martial skills. He had muscle strength but lacked the training to make it count. What good was he in the grand scale of things?

Cathal jerked to a seating position, slamming a fist on the soft mattress again. He remembered how Padraig had mentioned his training schedule—times of the day when he couldn't be with Cathal because he was training with Laoise. He chided himself for never having asked about it. But it wasn't too late.

"Padraig," he called, jumping to his feet and rushing to the front door. The young man was normally close by, doing whatever it was he did when he wasn't keeping him company. Sure enough, the tall Padraig came running through the doorway. "I have a question."

Cathal studied the young man. The boy was still growing into his long legs and often stumbled over his own feet. It was strange to think of him as a graceful swan when he was all legs and arms.

"Yes, Cathal?" Padraig's eyebrows arched.

"The training you go to every day, are they for some kind of martial training?" He remembered Eala mentioning the fact that they were a sect of warrior healers even though the only time he had seen them fight was when he had first come to the island. Of course, back then, Cathal hadn't known it was these gentle humans in the form of aggressive swans who had pecked at him with their hard beaks until he almost bled to death.

The boy nodded. "Sword and hand-to-hand combat training. Why do you ask?"

Cathal sighed. "I want to learn how to fight." His voice was steady and his chin high. "I want to be able to help you defend yourselves when you need it." And fight the king for Eala's freedom, but he kept that to himself.

If the boy was surprised by his request, he didn't show it. "I'll have to talk to Eala and Laoise, but it should be okay," he said. He wrinkled his brow. "Are you sure you want to do this? It's hard work, and you are still healing."

With a slap to his chest, Cathal guffawed. "Are you kidding me? I am in the best shape I've ever been. I could fight a dragon and win."

Padraig snorted. "Right. You have no clue how fierce and strong dragons are."

Cathal froze, his eyes widening. "You mean dragons are real?" If humans could turn into swans, why couldn't wyverns be just as real?

The boy burst out laughing, holding on to his middle. "Got you there, Cathal," he managed to say in between laughs.

Stone-faced, Cathal raised a single eyebrow. "I wouldn't dismiss the idea so quickly, young man," he quipped. "You've met my grandmother. How can you not believe dragons do indeed exist?"

Padraig laughed even harder. "I wonder what she would do if she knew you said that."

Cathal shrugged and cracked a smile. "Can you take me to Laoise right now? I will ask her myself." The sooner he started training, the sooner he could face the king and either kill him or die trying.

"WHAT are you plotting, *garmhac*?" Mhamó asked, her chin raised toward him, a squint in her eyes. "What are you really up to?"

Cathal threw her an innocent look. He had always been the lamb in the family, the one that took whatever came barreling at him with no complaints, never striving to break the ties of responsibility. It was only natural for his grandmother to be suspicious of this sudden wish to learn how to properly fight.

"I'm just bored, Mhamó, might as well learn something that may serve me well in the future." He hated lying to her, but he didn't want her to ask too many questions, to worry about what he may or may not do. "With Odhran in prison, I don't have to watch over him anymore. My whole schedule has opened up." He gave her what he hoped was a brilliant smile, the kind that always made him look younger. Instead, she scowled at him as if she knew he was hiding something. "No reason for you to worry about it. Drink your tea before it gets cold."

The old woman shook her head slightly and took a sip from the hot tea. "*Garmhac*, you must not do anything foolish," she warned, patting his knee. They were sitting next to each other at the round table in her room, drinking tea and snacking on tea cakes Lily Pad had brought them from the kitchen. The girl had left them alone to talk and wandered off with Padraig. "We already have an idiot in the family; we don't need two."

Her words might as well have been a bomb. Mhamó had never criticized his brother in any way other than sometimes calling him a foolish child. Had Cathal misunderstood her? "I never heard you talk like that about my brother."

Ó Broin threw a hand up in the air in disgust. "I know, Cathal, but it's about time, isn't it?" He would have laughed were he not confused by her words. "Stop being dense, child. Of course, I know your brother is cruel and immoral. Of course, I know how much you have suffered to keep him safe like you promised my daughter." She grabbed his hand and clutched it in hers. "It killed me, *garmhac*, every lowering of the whip, every day you spent behind bars because of that evil child, but like you, I'd made a promise that I must keep."

"Mom made you promise to keep him alive and well too?" Cathal couldn't imagine why his mother would have asked a frail old woman like Mhamó to do something like that.

She shook her head, looking older than a moment ago. "No, not your mother," she said in a tired voice. "Someone else. I do it for the future, Cathal, your future and the future of the common folk in this land."

Cathal knitted his brows, confused. What did she mean by that? Was Mhamó going senile? It hit him suddenly that he had no idea how old his grandmother was. She had always been old and hard of hearing, hadn't she? He couldn't recall her in any other way.

Except she seemed younger, more vibrant since she arrived at the island. He shook his head, dispelling the fancies dancing in his mind. She looked younger there because she didn't have to worry herself sick about food or about his brother getting himself in trouble again.

Memories of Mhamó shaking a wooden spoon and yelling at Odhran came rushing back. "You miscreant, evil child," she'd yell. "You better behave, or I will take you back to where you came from."

Cathal had always thought her choice of words to be funny. "Mhamó, you can't threaten him with something you can't possibly do. He won't take you seriously," he used to tell her.

"What are you laughing at, child?" his grandmother asked him. Cathal realized he had laughed out loud at his memories. Her dark eyes softened as a smile pulled at the corner of her lips. "But it's nice to hear you laugh again, *garmhac*, so wonderful."

He stretched across the tabletop and held on to her hand. "I'm happy here." Simple as pie.

Cara Ó Broin squeezed his hand and winked. It was such an uncharacteristic thing for her, Cathal started. "You like her, don't you?"

His mouth went dry, and his cheeks caught fire. "Who?" He knew perfectly well who she meant, but he wasn't comfortable talking about his love life with his grandmother.

She pulled on his hand, let it go, and then slapped

it playfully. "Silly boy, who else? The lovely Queen of the Swans. She's the one you saved ten years ago, isn't she?"

If he weren't sitting down, he would most likely fall because his legs turned to jelly in surprise. "H-how do y-you know that?"

"It's a long story that involves you thinking I am older and deafer than I really am," she said, utterly deadpan. Cathal felt unreasonably guilty for those thoughts even though, at the time, they seemed to fit. "Child, don't feel bad. I wanted you to think that. It's all part of my wicked plan." She rubbed her hands together like a witch in one of those street plays they often watched growing up.

"Mhamó, stop that. You're scaring me." It was hard for Cathal to recognize this playful, much more youthful woman before him. It was as if his grandmother had gone through some strange metamorphosis. Had the swans done their magic on her? No, Eala had said that she was the only one who could make someone younger. But the fact remained, Mhamó looked and acted years younger than when he had last seen her.

"Relax, Cathal. You are young, and yet you carry the weight of the world on your shoulders," she said with such love in her voice and gaze, Cathal immediately calmed down. "I hope that one day you can have everything that you deserve. I won't rest until you do."

The one question that Cathal had carried around

most of his life percolated to the surface for the first time in a long while, and before he could stop himself, he asked, "Who was my father? And Odhran's?"

He had long suspected they didn't have the same father since Cathal had brown hair and eyes the color of hazelnuts while his brother was fair and blue-eyed. Where he was tall and slim, Odhran was short and stocky. Then, there was the eleven-year age difference between them.

The old woman didn't seem surprised by the question. "Your father—and Odhran's—is better forgotten, child," she said, clicking her tongue. "There are men who should never have children. Odhran's is one of them."

Now that the question was out in the open, Cathal was not about to let the matter lie. "But Mom always spoke tenderly of him." She'd never once mentioned his name, but she claimed him to be a man of noble birth, someone who could make their lives easier. If that was the truth, it never crystallized into anything at all.

Mhamó sighed deeply and locked her dark eyes on his. "Your mother—my daughter—was not well, I think you know that," she said. Yes, part of him had always known that his mother was what many called soft in the head. She was a beautiful, graceful woman who doted on Odhran like a little girl caring for a baby doll. She'd rock him for hours, singing lullabies and dancing around the room, her gaze fixed on some faraway place no one else could see. "When she was pregnant with you, Odhran's father tried to kill her." Cathal's heart lurched. "He left her for dead, but when I found her, she was still alive. However, she had lost most of her wits. She was never the same again."

How come he had never known about this? Something twisted inside him. His life was shrouded in lies or, at least, untold truths. What else did he not know? What else was buried and waiting to be dug up? "Why did you never tell me?"

Grandma's face opened into a sad smile. "Because it wouldn't have made a difference, would it?" she asked with irritating logic. "You worshiped my daughter, and, in her madness, she was happy too. Why stir up the shit from the past? I knew I would tell you one day when it was time."

"But, Mhamó, I've been protecting my brother because of a promise I made to a delusional woman—" He knew even as he spoke that he would have done it anyway. He loved his mother and would do anything for her.

"That promise, child, was the only thing your mother did right. You will find out why in due time." The old woman stood up and brushed her hands over the front of her dress. "Take me on a walk, will you? That wicked Lily Pad has been too busy making googly eyes at Padraig and has forsaken me." She chuckled. "Ah, to be young and in love again."

Cathal offered his arm for support and stared at

her with concern. Had she ever been in love? And if so, who had been the man who captured her heart? A question for another day, Cathal thought.

Or maybe never.

CHAPTER FOURTEEN

Wishes

She wondered whether he did it out of a misguided sense of duty or some other weird masochist reason she couldn't fathom. Each sporadic visit to his brother was obviously pure torture for Cathal, and yet, she knew he'd go back. Once he had realized Cathal was unwilling to help him escape, Odhran took special pains to make each visit unforgettable.

"Don't let him frazzle you, Cathal," Eala told him as they walked into the cell room. He no longer asked her to leave; her presence seemed to be comforting to him, a backup of sorts even if only in spirit. His brother was an expert at emotional blackmail. After talking to him, Cathal couldn't do much more than crash into bed and, by the looks of him in the morning, toss and turn all night. Odhran's gift to find and push his brother's every button would have been admirable if it wasn't wicked.

Odhran was lying on the floor, hands behind his neck, legs crossed at the ankles. Without bothering to spare them a glance, he said, "If it's not my beloved brother and his bitch."

Cathal's face turned instantly scarlet, but he managed to keep his voice calm and leveled. "I told you before not to address Her Majesty that way."

His brother did turn his face in their direction then. "Or what? She'll kill me?" He barked a laugh. "She'll kill me anyway, so what difference does it make?" Could he not even contemplate that it was possible to be shown mercy? Of course, he couldn't, for he had no heart. How could the same mother have birthed two boys so utterly different? One a beautiful soul and the other a creature of darkness. "What do you want? Came to gloat about your freedom?"

Cathal would never do such a thing, but he didn't say it. "Just came to check on you and make sure you're okay."

Odhran sprang to a sitting position and laughed. "You're hilarious, my brother. Okay? Oh yes, I'm fabulous. I'm stuck in a prison cell, surrounded by idiots who want me dead. What could be better?"

"They haven't killed you yet, Odhran," Cathal said, stepping forward. "You should be grateful."

In one fluid movement that belied his short legs, Cathal's brother got on his feet and bowed. "I am eternally grateful to you and your bitch," he said, voice low and threatening. Anticipating his reaction, Eala stepped closer and held on to Cathal's hand. It didn't go unnoticed. "You're fucking her! What do you know, the goody-two-shoes has a wild side."

Eala held on tighter. "Don't take the bait," she whispered, gluing her body to Cathal's back. "He wants you to lose control."

A disturbing smile stretched on Odhran's lips. "How is it? To fuck a queen, I mean." He chortled. "Oh wait, you have nothing to compare it with other than your own hand, right brother? Poor lonely boy could never find a hole for his peg."

Cathal pulled hard on her hand. "Let me beat the shit out of him, please," he grunted. "I'm ashamed to call him my brother."

"No, that's what he wants," Eala told him, holding him steady. "He wants you to break the barrier by throwing yourself at it. Not only will it not work, but it will probably kill you. Don't listen to him."

His shoulders slowly relaxed, even if his breathing was still rapid and rugged. "You're right, Eala. He does not deserve my anger." He turned around to face her. "Let's go."

Hand in hand, they headed back to the entrance, ignoring the barrage of insults trailing behind them. Cathal's hand trembled in hers. Her heart broke for him. How could his brother, whom he had taken care of and protected his whole life, attack him with such odious words? Her heart overflowed with an overwhelming need to hold and comfort him. How she'd love to do just that, to fuse her lips to his, let her bare skin melt against him, but she couldn't. She shouldn't have even kissed him. That gift of hers worked without any bidding from her. A simple kiss caused a flow of her healing energy to escape her. She could only hope it had been negligible and that the king wouldn't notice on her next visit to the palace. If he so much as suspected anything, he would bring his soldiers to the island and search every nook and cranny until he found Cathal.

"Let's go to the lake," Cathal said, pulling her down the path that led to the closest bank. "A swim will do me good."

She couldn't argue with that. Her next visit to the king was quickly approaching, and she welcomed any distraction. They dashed to the lake as if afraid they may not get there on time and swiftly shed their outwear.

Cathal jumped in first, and for a moment, she indulged in shameless voyeurism as he swam away from the bank, the muscles in his back rippling as he moved through the water with powerful strokes. She had tried to squelch it, that little spark of hope his grandmother had lit inside her, but at moments like this, that wee flame erupted into a tundra fire. Could it be possible? Could it be that the loathsome young man in the prison cell was the key to their freedom? Eala was afraid to wish for what she could not have, but Ó

Broin had given her a reason to dream of being with the man she had come to love.

"Are you going to just stand there?" Cathal yelled out, a few feet away from the water's edge.

She laughed and took off, running to the small ledge that jutted out from the rock before flipping in the air and diving headfirst into the clear, cool water of the lake. If only life could be this simple and fun all the time.

LIKE children, they sat on the floor by the empty hearth, feasting on the snacks Laoise had brought them earlier. The plates of pastries and roasted nuts littered the marble floor between them, and Eala couldn't stop wondering how wonderful it would be if they could do this every day for the rest of their lives.

Cathal leaned against the wall, his long legs stretched out in front of him, munching away at the treats. She watched him as he closed his eyes and moaned a little every time he took another bite. There was such pleasure in his expression, such delight that it brought joy to her heart. He had lived such a deprived life, deprived of good food, of protection, of love. The loss of his mother when he was such a wee bairn must have been devastating, even though it seemed as if in her mental confusion she'd been more concerned about Odhran than her oldest son. Grandma had never been able to fill that void in his life. The old woman had told her carrying the secret she did had not been easy, but sacrifices had to be made for the good of all.

"What would you wish your life was like?" Cathal asked suddenly, a cream puff still churning in his mouth. "If you could pick, I mean. What do you wish for?"

Eala paused to think, a flaky pastry in her hand, frozen halfway to her mouth. She tilted her head and sighed. "What's the point of dreaming the impossible?"

The sadness she had become an expert at keeping at bay now rushed through her. After years of protecting herself and her thoughts with a wall of ice, she found that Cathal had cracked that wall; first, when they had met ten years ago and he showed her a kindness she had forgotten existed, and now—she had to stop these wishful, foolish feelings before anyone got hurt.

Cathal reached out to her free hand. "Indulge me. Nothing wrong with dreaming." She didn't agree with that. There was too much to lose by dreaming about what you couldn't have. "Pretend for a moment that nothing bad could possibly happen if you were to have your wishes. What would it be like?"

She hesitated again. "My swans would be free of danger and could fly wherever they wanted to and do what they were born to do: take care of the sick," she replied after a while.

Cathal shook his head. "No, not for your people, for you." His golden eyes seemed to shimmer, burrowing into hers. "What would you want *your* life to be like?"

It came out unbidden as if it had been waiting for the right opportunity to be released. "I'd live in a small cottage by the ocean, fly and swim every day, and then sleep—" *in the arms of the one I love.* Cathal's arms promised the peace and bliss she dreamed of but couldn't have. She cleared her throat. "You?"

"Same," he said with a generous smile, the kind that always made her weak in the knees. "But I want you by my side." Her heart stopped for a second before setting out in a race. "I want to hold you at night while you sleep and make love to you when you're awake." He cupped her cheek with his hand. "I want to swim in the ocean with you and watch you fly over the waves." He leaned over, his face closer to hers. "I want to be able to kiss you without the fear of hurting you and your people."

Just as their lips were about to touch, Eala pulled back, suddenly aware of reality, their reality. "But we can't," she whispered in a strangled voice. "We can't, Cathal."

If she didn't already feel broken enough inside, the way Cathal's face fell and his eyes misted shattered the last of her. His shoulders slumped, and he dropped his chin to his chest, his hand slack. "It's always been like this for me, Eala," he breathed so softly, she had to strain to hear it. "But I never cared before. Until now.

This kick in the groin from the universe really hit the spot, my Queen."

She didn't know what to say. What *could* she say? They were both insignificant pawns in a greater-than-life game. An overwhelming urge to tell him what Ó Broin had said came over her. Wouldn't it be better if he could understand why his mother and his grandmother did what they did? Wouldn't it be comforting to know why he had to suffer his whole life for a brother who didn't deserve it? Most importantly, wouldn't it give him hope? She shook her head. No, there was no point in sowing that seed in his heart when the outcome was still uncertain. What if all the carefully planned future went terribly wrong? No, she couldn't do that to him. There were only a couple months to go; she'd wait.

Her hand twisted inside his, and she squeezed tighter. "I love you," she blurted out the confession and froze. This was so unlike her, this impulsive woman who didn't weigh the consequences of her words before spitting them out. Cathal raised his eyes to hers, mouth ajar. She gulped and repeated, "I love you, Cathal." There was less fervor but much more conviction this time.

Cathal hesitated for a moment as if processing her words but then drew her into his arms in a tight embrace. She had never felt so safe, so cherished as she did now. His body heat mingling with hers, her head resting on the flat of his shoulder, his hot breath on her skin…could they stay like that forever? Forget about their responsibilities and the world around them and just drink in each other.

"I love you too, Eala," Cathal whispered against her forehead. "I've loved you even before I knew you were human." He chuckled softly. "You, as a swan, were my only friend who knew things about me that no one else did. I loved you even then."

The time for her next palace visit was rapidly approaching, but for now, she had Cathal's arms around her, the sound of his heartbeat in her ears, and the feeling of total joy inside her heart. Tomorrow always came, but for the moment, they both had today.

CHAPTER FIFTEEN

Shadows

Cathal

The shadows came out of nowhere. One moment, Eala's blue-green eyes sparkled like stars; a blink later, they were muted by darkness. It was as if her soul had left her body. Cathal didn't know what to do. Should he ask her about it, or was it too early in their relationship to intrude in what could be a personal matter?

"Morning, Cathal." Fully recovered now, Cathal didn't need Padraig's services anymore, but the young man still came every day and kept him company until such time as they both had to go to training.

Since Laoise had given her permission for Cathal to join her warriors in martial training, he hadn't missed a single session. Maybe it was all wishful thinking, but he could have sworn his muscles bulged further, and he could run farther and harder than ever. For the first time in his life, he felt healthy. Not that he had been a sickly boy, but he had been in a permanent state of exhaustion for most of his years. Now he felt refreshed, relaxed, and almost certain he could take on the world.

He wondered whether Padraig knew why Eala had suddenly lost her spark. "Why is the queen looking so distant?" He watched the boy with interest, not wanting to miss any reaction to his question.

The young man's smile died on his lips. "It's almost time for her to visit the palace," he said, shoulders slumping. "Her soul always goes into a hidden place inside of her mind this time, every month. She thinks we don't notice, but we do. We all feel guilty that she must pay the price for our safety."

Cathal's stomach churned. Of course, how could he have forgotten about it? He had been so involved with his own happiness that he had selfishly forgotten that his queen would have to subject herself to the lascivious king once again. Familiar helplessness filled him, red hot anger boiling in his chest and gut, burning him from the inside out.

"There must be something we can do to stop it." As he said it, he knew there wasn't. Wouldn't her people have done it already? But he couldn't accept it without a fight. The thought of the monarch's filthy hands on Eala made him violently sick. He gagged. "We *have* to do something."

Padraig lowered his eyes. "We are willing to do

whatever it takes, even die if necessary, to stop her from being used like this," he said, his voice catching a few times. "But she won't let us. Her sense of duty won't let us take the risk."

"You're a warrior people. Why can't you fight against the king?" He didn't mean to sound accusatory, but his aching heart spoke louder than his head.

"There are only twelve of us," Padraig whispered. "There are thousands of them. Even the king's personal guard has over a hundred men. What can twelve of us do against that? In the end, he would kill us all and take Eala captive."

Padraig was right. It was a hopeless situation. For a moment, Cathal wished he was brave and skilled enough to sneak into the palace and kill the king. Funny how he had never thought of killing before, and yet, now, those thoughts crossed his mind constantly. His need to protect the woman he loved was stirring up feelings and urges he had never experienced before.

"When is she going?" He couldn't accept it. He couldn't.

"In three days, she'll go into seclusion to make sure her healing power is fully recharged." To prepare herself mentally and emotionally for what she was about to do, most likely. "Then, a couple days later, she'll fly to Nem and stay for a couple days."

If he couldn't control the beating of his own heart, he was going to explode. He couldn't breathe, he couldn't think, his fingers had gone numb. How could he watch her go into the greedy arms of the king and not do anything? But what could he do? Fretting about it would only add to her anxiety, her shame. He couldn't do that to her. He had to be strong for her sake. Cathal was not sure he could do it, though.

"I have to talk to her," Cathal said, standing up suddenly, almost sending the small teacup tumbling across the tabletop. Padraig looked alarmed, his eyes wide open and fingers tightly knotted around his cup. "I have to."

Cathal was already out the door when he heard the young man's voice yell out behind him, "But she's working right now." Cathal paused for a moment until his companion offered, a tinge of hope in his voice, "In her quarters. She's working in her rooms."

That was all the information he needed. Cathal uttered a silent thank you to Padraig and took off running toward Eala's dwelling. It wasn't far—nothing on the island seemed far—and mere minutes later, he was knocking on the side of her open door. She didn't answer, so he knocked again, this time louder.

"Who is it?" Her voice was strained. Had she been crying?

"It's me, Cathal," he said, hand braced on the door jamb. "May I come in?" There was silence. He fought the urge to walk in, but he couldn't, not without her permission. "Please. Eala, I need to talk to you."

After another long quiet moment, she said, "Come on in, Cathal."

He didn't wait a second and walked in, closing the door behind him. She was sitting at the table, looking through a pile of notebooks; her fingers were stained with blue ink and her cheeks with tears. He released a loud breath, the need to draw her into his arms so strong, he held on to the back of a chair to stop himself.

She peered up at him, shiny eyes betraying the pain he was sure she'd rather hide from him, and smiled weakly. "I'm busy with the books, Cathal," she said without conviction. "What do you need?"

Cathal pulled the chair closer to her and sat, their knees touching. "I need you to be happy."

He didn't know whether it was his words or something else, but she broke, crying. The uncontrollable sobs escaped through the fingers of her hand as she folded in over herself. He stood up and kneeled before her, his hands on her knees, shaking with the knowledge there was nothing he could do to help her.

"Don't cry, Eala," he pleaded, gently rubbing the top of her thighs. "Let me hold you at least. I won't do anything. I just want to comfort you."

Much to his surprise, her arms went around his neck, and she fell to her knees too, crushing him against her in a desperate embrace. "I'm sorry, Cathal, I shouldn't be crying."

He wrapped his arms around her, brushing his lips on the side of her neck. "What are you apologizing for, my Queen? If anyone has the right to cry her heart out,

it's you," he whispered, fingers weaving through her thick red hair. "Cry if that helps, cry until you have no tears left. I will hold and support you." Her sobs intensified, but she relaxed in his arms. "I will love you forever. One day, I will find a way to end your pain."

It was a promise he fully intended to keep.

MHAMÓ had the same look Cathal had come to identify with the words, "You're in so much trouble, young man." Except this time, neither he nor his brother was the target of her anger. With Eala in seclusion for the past few days, Cathal spent a lot of time with his grandmother while Padraig wooed the young and pretty Lily Pad. In retrospect, maybe telling Mhamó about Eala's sacrifice had not been the best idea.

"That weasel of a king!" she spat out with such heat, Cathal could have sworn smoke followed her words. "Good-for-nothing bastard. The lives that have been destroyed so he can have his way. Rian, your days are numbered."

It was unsettling to hear her talk about the king as if they had grown up together. "Mhamó, you shouldn't talk about the king like that," he said, throwing worried glances at the door. "There are royal guards on the island. What if they hear you?"

She blasted him with her sharp eyes. "Don't be a fool, *garmhac*. If that asshole finds out we're here, we're all dead. Why would I worry about a few words?"

Cathal noticed, not for the first time, how his grandmother's dark eyes were no longer those of an old woman. Instead, there was a fire and vitality to them that defied all odds. The wisdom of ages was still reflected there, but now the spark of youth mixed and mingled with it.

"There's nothing we can do about it." The truth in his voice crushed him in defeat. He had not slept in days, his mind too busy searching for a way—any way—to stop the cruel game Nem's ruler was playing. All he got was a whole lot of nothing. "Tomorrow, she'll be gone again to be broken by him, and I will be here waiting to help her put herself together again. What good am I when I cannot protect the woman I love? What useless life I've led, protecting my brother who does not deserve to be protected, but there's nothing I can do to help Eala."

Mhamó stepped closer and draped an arm over his shoulders in an uncharacteristic gesture. "Boy, your life has never been and never will be useless," she whispered, patting his arm with her other hand. "There are things that you don't know, things to come that will change the world as we know it, and *you* play a big role in it." Cathal started, turning his face to her. "Many secrets will be revealed, but for now, rest assured that your life is not useless. Much to the contrary."

"What do you mean? What secrets?" What kind of secrets could his poor and tiny family hold? Mom's mental health problems had never been a secret. And Grandma? Could it be that the woman whom he remembers as always old and hard of hearing had been hiding something all this time?

The old woman's smile never reached her eyes. She patted his arm again. "You'll find out when the time is right, child. Until then, just be who you are and stop blaming yourself for all the woes of this world." She let him go and sighed. "You're a good man, Cathal; you're a very good man."

That might be, but Cathal felt worthless, helpless. He dropped to a nearby chair and let out a loud exhale. "For all it's worth, Mhamó, for all it's worth." At that moment, he wished he was more like his brother, reckless and cruel, able to come up with a wicked plan to kill the king. Deep down inside, however, he doubted he would ever be able to kill anyone.

The next day came too quickly. Cathal barely slept, tossing in bed all night haunted by the knowledge of what Eala was about to do. Every time he closed his eyes, images of her in the king's arms assailed him, as toxic and corroding as acid. By morning, he felt as if his insides had been burned to a crisp and melted into nothing. The void should not have hurt, but it did. It consumed every vital organ, every bit of his consciousness, and stirred up such wrath as he had never felt before.

He had promised Eala not to see her off, but, in the end, he couldn't do it. He had to see her, hold her in his arms, let her know that someone loved her more than life itself. As soon as dawn broke, Cathal ran all the way to the water's edge, where she told him she'd be taking flight and waited. Just as the sun was rising behind the hills, his queen appeared around the bend. Even in a plain shift with no adornments of any kind, Eala was easily the most beautiful woman he had ever seen. She had not bothered with her hair, combing it into a top bun, and there were no shoes on her feet.

"Cathal!" She stopped suddenly, her swollen eyes opened wide and her body rigid. "What are you doing here?"

He didn't waver. He crossed the short space between them and wrapped her in a fierce hug, his face buried in the crook of her neck. "I'm sorry. I know I promised not to come, but I needed to see you and tell you how much I love you."

Hesitantly at first, Eala's hands came around Cathal and locked behind his back, pressing him closer. "I don't want you to see me like this," she cried against the side of his face. "I'm so ashamed."

Cathal pulled her away, holding onto her shoulders, and searched for her gaze. "You have nothing to be ashamed of, my Queen," he declared. "You're doing what you must to protect your people. Your sacrifice is nothing shameful."

They held each other for a while, but then Eala

pulled away. "I have to go." Her choked words scratched at his heart. "I will be back as soon as I have recovered my strength."

There were many things he wanted to say to her, but nothing seemed to be right at that moment. So, he let her go. He watched as she stepped back, turned to the lake, and opened her arms. In seconds, the beautiful, majestic swan he had cared for ten years ago was standing where Eala had been, powerful wings wide open, ready to fly. At the last moment, the swan turned her graceful neck to look at him, and what he saw in those eyes burned a hole in his very soul.

Why was he so useless?

CHAPTER SIXTEEN
The Temple

Eala

The world hadn't stopped.

No matter how many times Eala went through it, that small fact always surprised her. Despite the pain, the shame, and the feeling of being soiled inside and out, the world kept going. Sequestered in her house, Eala's eyes followed the rays of light that, despite all odds, managed to break through the barriers of the closed shutters and doors of her room. She knew hiding wouldn't change a thing; she'd still carry this stain. But with each visit to the king, it took her longer to recover, as if the more healing power she bestowed on him, however unwilling, the less life energy she was left with. She'd been back for three days and still couldn't find the strength to get out of bed and face the others. Face Cathal.

A soft knock on the door yanked her back from her dazed state. "Yes?" Was that really her voice? Weak and shaky like that of an old woman.

"My Queen, I have some food." Good and reliable Laoise, the only person on the island she was willing to face after her monthly ordeal. "I'm coming in."

The door creaked open, letting the resilient sunlight flood in. Eala blinked and covered her eyes with her arm. "I'm not hungry, Laoise."

The older woman closed the door behind her and crossed the space between them to set down the tray she carried. "Nonsense, you need to regain your strength back." Laoise sounded like a mother. Eala supposed she had been the closest to one since her teacher had passed. Laoise was just a few years older than herself but had a motherly quality that made all the other swans rely on her for comfort and guidance. "And how are you going to get any better without sunshine?" She sounded outraged, and Eala almost laughed.

Eala watched Laoise open all the shutters and drench the house in warm, bright light. The sun had always brightened her spirits, but not now. In fact, seeing all that beautiful light made her sadder, a reminder of what life could have been if she hadn't fallen for the king's tricks.

Laoise helped her sit up and fed her the hot ginseng chicken soup she had brought with her, one spoonful at a time. "This will boost your qi, my Queen." Eala found the strength to smile. No matter how many times she told Laoise to call her by her first name, the woman still reverted to the more formal address. "Cathal is very worried about you," she added after a pause.

Eala's breath caught. There was a war raging inside of her. The need to see him, to seek solace in his arms and kind smile vied with the shame of facing the man she loved after what she had done. "I'm not worthy of him, Laoise. How can I look him in the eye?"

"Don't be dumb," Laoise exclaimed, her lips turned into an angry grimace. "Who can possibly be more worthy than the one who has sacrificed everything to protect her people? Besides, he obviously loves you, and you love him. What's there to be afraid of?"

There was much to fear, but Laoise was right; after all, Cathal was gentle and kind, and he was well acquainted with shame and pain. "Help me get dressed and then call him here, will you?"

Laoise clapped her hands and smiled. "Yes, my Queen."

In no time, her old friend had her dressed in a simple long sheath the color of sunshine that left her ivory shoulders bare beneath a translucent golden shawl. She didn't bother putting on shoes, and Laoise was determined to leave her hair free of ornaments—a short cascade of loose coppery curls that barely touched her shoulders. She left Eala sitting at the table with a comforting pot of ginger tea and a flutter in her heart. Despite the pain, a small kernel of joy had burst inside her at the thought of being with Cathal again. Was that what love did for you? Heal all wounds?

Cathal crossed the front door only a few minutes later. The black crisscross shirt he wore over his loose white pants and the beads of moisture on his forehead told her he'd been training. He was slimly built but had strong shoulders and powerful biceps. Even before he started his workouts, he'd had the body of a survivor. After all, he couldn't have protected his idiot brother all this time without developing some muscle. Now, after weeks of a strict regime of exercise under the sun, his earlier paleness and weakness were gone. There was a new determination and confidence in the way Cathal walked toward her. It made her smile.

He dashed across to fall on his knees by her, clutching her cold hands in his. "You're freezing," he exclaimed, alarm rounding his eyes. He dropped her hands and stood up to refill her cup with hot tea. "Here, drink more."

Eala obeyed with a tremulous smile. "I can feel myself warming up already, now that you're here," she said, setting the cup down and seeking his hands. He wrapped them in his and rubbed them gently. "You're looking stronger with each passing day."

His smile brought the sun inside. "Laoise is a ruthless master," he quipped, still stroking her hands. "Padraig took pity on me and has been helping me catch up. How can your swans look so graceful and be so tough?"

She laughed, the sound strangely soothing to her

own ears. "We have to compensate for the awkward long necks and short legs." Surprised with her own joke, she let out a loud bark of a laugh, belatedly muffling it with a hand.

Cathal's smile grew wider. He was handsome, but she doubted he realized that. She knew that in the normal world, most women were blinded by status and might; they would have totally overlooked someone like him. Their loss. He had a heart and a soul to match his looks.

"Would you like to go on a walk?" he asked, eyebrows raised in perfect arches. "It's beautiful out, and you know what they say about the sun's rays, don't you?" Eala shook her head. "A sun's ray keeps sadness at bay."

Sweet Cathal. "Not sure I have the strength to walk," she confessed, looking down at her legs.

"No problem," Cathal said. In an unexpected move, he slid one arm under her knees and another under her arms and swooped her off the chair. She let out a tiny gasp. "See? I told you Laoise has been ruthless. But my muscles thank her." He winked at her, his bright brown eyes so close to her, they blurred a bit. "Shall we go outside?"

Eala nodded, draping her arm around his neck for stability. "This is a first," she said. "No one has ever carried me like this."

Cathal was already crossing to the door when he stopped and peered at her. "Not true," he said, serious

all of a sudden. "I once carried you just like this ten years ago." How could she have forgotten that? She had been half-conscious, but she remembered his body heat against her feathers, how his hands had gently held her to his chest. "We came full circle, it seems."

That damned resilient and stubborn flame of hope stretched a smile on her lips. Maybe they were fated together. Maybe, just maybe, the Guardians had something better in store for them. She lowered her head to his shoulder as he quietly carried her out into the sunshine and made her fall deeper in love with him.

EALA couldn't remember the last time she had visited the small temple nestled in the wildest part of the island. She had never questioned its location, considering they all lived in a magic floating island which in itself was odd enough. But as she stood there that day, staring at the half-hidden entrance to the cave that housed the Temple of the Guardians, she wondered how her people, how this island ever came to be. The Swan People had been around for centuries, their origins lost in the mists of time. As far as she knew, the island had always been her people's home for half of the year, under the dubious protection of the Guardians until the King of Nem decided otherwise. There had been a time, she remembered, when she came to the temple every week when on the island, her small hand caught in her master's firm grip. They had lit candles at the altar, kneeled on the cold stone floor, and prayed in a language long forgotten. She might have known what the words meant at some point, but their meaning had been lost to her throughout the years.

Laoise had brought a sharp blade and was enthusiastically cutting down the brush that covered the entrance, the swooshing and chomping sounds of the blade against greenery and branches a wild symphony breaking the silence of the morning. After a while, she stopped, wiped her hands on her dress, and declared it done.

"Should I stay with you, my Queen?" Laoise asked, a stolen glance in Eala's direction.

Eala shook her head. "No, thank you, Laoise. I think I'd like a minute alone with the Guardians."

The older woman left, the sword dangling from one hand, slowing down up the path to look back at her queen. Sweet Laoise, always worried about her, but there was nothing to worry about. She had been dreaming of the temple, about the times she had accompanied her master here and how peaceful it had always made her feel. She could use some of that peace now; therefore, she came, hoping to find it there.

After a few moments, Eala entered the cave. Even though all candles had long been extinguished, there was a soft glow inside, just bright enough to illuminate her path. The temple was not large or deep. All it took was a few steps inside, and she was standing before the altar, a long, narrow stone slab on top of two giant rocks. Against all logic, the neglected temple was free of dust, and the altar looked as if someone had been wiping it regularly. The two iron containers where the thin candles were placed shone in the dim glow of whatever magic produced it. Had one of her swans been sneaking in here and cleaning it? She couldn't imagine who. Most of them were younger than herself and unaware of the temple's existence.

"Amazing how it keeps by itself, isn't it?" Eala spun around, hands up in a defensive stance toward the unexpected visitor. "Hello, my Queen. Sorry if I startled you." Cathal's grandmother stood behind her, looking less and less like an old woman. "I hope you don't mind my company."

As surprised as Eala was by the other woman's sudden appearance, she couldn't be upset. She liked Cara Ó Broin, her white hair belying her dark raven looks. "Of course, I don't mind. I'm just surprised to see you here." She squinted against the dimness. "How did you know about this place?"

Ó Broin laughed. Was her back straighter than before? "I'm much older than I look," she said. "I know things which have been forgotten by most." Eala tilted her head. What could she possibly mean? If anything, and defying all odds, the woman appeared younger and younger with each passing day. "Don't look at me like that. Why would the queen of a magical species be surprised that there are others out there with similar secrets?"

"Are you saying you are a magical creature too?" That would account for the strange changes in her these past few weeks.

The woman smiled and sighed. "That's exactly what I'm saying," she said. "Except, there aren't as many of my people as there are of yours." There were only twelve of the swans left. How many exactly were there of Ó Broin's kind? "As far as I know, I'm the last of my kind. Except for my grandson, of course, but he is not full-blooded."

Eala actually stumbled in shock. Cathal was a magical creature? "What are you saying?" Sweet Cathal couldn't look any more human. How could it be?

"He doesn't know, and to be honest, I'm not sure how much magic he has in him other than being the wonderful man he is." Eala wouldn't argue with her there. His smile definitely held magic. "My daughter was not full-blooded either; therefore, the magic in him has been pretty diluted, but he is—at least in a small measure—one of my kind."

"What kind are you?" It had to be asked. Eala had never heard of any other magical species still roaming this world. "How come Cathal doesn't know about it?"

Cara sighed again and stole a glance at the altar.

There were no statues on it, just a simple stone plaque with the words "Guardians Keep Us" that stood between the two candle containers. "Shall we light a candle or two?"

As curious as Eala was, she nodded and turned to the altar again. Hanging from one side of it, there was a small wooden pot packed with the thin sticks of wax used as candles in the temple. She grabbed three, lit them with the matches she had brought with her, and stuck them in the sand within the containers. From a corner of her eye, she watched as Cara did the same in the other container. They both fell to their knees onto the cold but strangely clean, round pads on the floor and lowered their heads for a silent prayer. The long-forgotten sense of peace these visits used to bring flooded through Eala's body and soul. Like a cold wave washing over the hot sands of the beach, the peace swallowed her whole. She heard a whimper and realized it was hers.

"How long it's been, Eala?" Cathal's grandmother asked, still kneeling beside her.

"Too long, it seems." It was the honest truth. "I haven't been here since our queen passed."

"Ah yes, Queen Aoibhe," Cara said. Eala snapped her head around to face her. "Yes, I knew her. She was a great woman and a wonderful queen. She was missed."

"How do you know my master?" After so many years of not being surprised by anything, Eala barely knew how to react.

"You've met me before too, Eala, when you were very little," Cara said with a sad smile. "After all, we children of the Guardians used to stick together like glue. That was before Rian's great grandfather's reign and the Great Cleansing."

Eala searched her memories for any knowledge of what the Great Cleansing was. It rang a bell, but she couldn't quite pin it down. "What was that?"

Cara let out a bitter laugh. "You know it as the Great Massacre," she said. Eala's stomach churned. Yes, she knew what that was. It had happened long before she was born but was still taught to every swan. "King Darragh, Rian's great grandfather, was a cruel man who feared anything that he couldn't comprehend or control."

The story went that Darragh took a sudden dislike of magic creatures and decided to exterminate them. Many species were burnt alive, others poisoned or starved. A small group of Swan people had been able to escape to their elusive floating island, but most others had perished.

"There was a reprieve during the long reigns of both Rian's grandfather and father, so a few remnants were able to exist in hiding," Cara continued. "My people were one of them. Unfortunately, our bloodline has been diluted throughout the years; after I pass, that will be it for the great race of witches."

"You're a witch?"

Witches were the stuff of legend. There were many

stories around the mythological species of humans born with exceptional magical talents. Some bordered on the ridiculous, portraying witches as old hags who flew on brooms and wore wide brim pointy hats. Others painted them in a more realistic way, however maybe not any kinder. And, of course, there was the legend of King Rian's only son and heir who had been spawned by a witch and cursed at birth. Eala wondered if there was any truth to that story and if indeed such a child existed. In all her visits to the palace, she had yet to meet the sole heir to the throne, who should be about to turn eighteen years old very soon.

"The last of my kind," Cara said. "Thankfully, we witches live very long lives. I will outlive that evil king by many years, no matter how much energy he consumes from you." The old woman touched Eala's shoulder. "My Queen, you will get your revenge, I promise. It won't be long now."

Eala was not set on revenge. All she wanted was peace and the freedom to not have to subjugate to the king's sexual demands. She wanted to be by Cathal's side and live a quiet life on the island with all her swans. She told Cara as much.

Ó Broin smiled. "I know, Eala, I know you do not seek revenge," she said, her voice lowered to a whisper. "But I do. Not for myself but for all the poor women who suffered under Rian's hands, their families, my daughter, and my grandson." Eala wondered why Cathal's grandmother rarely mentioned Odhran. He was, after all, her grandson as well. Cara looked up at the plaque on the altar. "The Guardians want revenge for all the lives recklessly lost because of one man's greed. He will answer for his crimes."

She had to ask, "And Odhran?"

A raven glance came to rest on Eala's. "Odhran will also pay for his crimes. They say that the apple never falls too far from the tree, don't they?"

CHAPTER SEVENTEEN

Yule

Cathal

"Does it ever get cold on the island?" Cathal asked Padraig as they sat by the water, enjoying the waning heat of the sun. He had been there for a few months and hadn't noticed any change in the weather. By his calculations, it should be December already, and yet, there was no hint of winter.

The young man spit out the reed he had been chewing on. "Sometimes, but not often. It is mostly spring all year round."

Cathal squinted against the sunshine. "Sometimes? How does that work?"

Padraig shrugged. "Not sure," he said. "I never asked."

With a shake of the head, Cathal patted the boy in the back. "I never felt as old as I do at this moment, my friend," he said with a low chuckle. "You were not even a little curious as to why and how that happens?"

A familiar female voice answered in Padraig's stead, "The boy was born and grew up on the island and has known nothing else. He wouldn't think it was strange."

Eala, beautiful as always in a blue ethereal robe, joined them, slinking down to the grass where they were sitting.

"You look beautiful," Cathal whispered, yearning catching fire inside him. Padraig guffawed, earning him a slap on the shoulder from the other man.

"The Guardians decide when to change the weather," she explained. "Even I don't know why or how it's done, but once in a while, we get a snowy day. Otherwise, we get spring with sunshine, warmth, and rain." She looked at him, her eyebrows raised. "Why? Are you bored with the good weather?"

Cathal shook his head and laughed. "No, of course not. I enjoy not being frozen to the bone." In an instant, memories of winters past where he had walked around for days half-frozen, never being able to warm up, flooded in. "I like being warm. I was simply trying to get my bearings, timewise. It's December now, right?"

The queen nodded. "Yule is upon us in just over a week," she said. "We must prepare for a feast."

Time seemed suspended on the island. Days and nights passed, but it was as if time itself didn't budge. Yule was around the corner. "Odhran's birthday is coming," he exclaimed. He had almost forgotten. "My mother always said he was born with one foot in December and the other in January."

"Your grandmother said she has something planned for his birthday," Eala said with her usual tilt of the head. "Do you know what it is?"

It was the first time Cathal had heard that. "She didn't mention anything to me. Back home, we were always too poor to celebrate anything. I tried to bring in some sweets or pastries from town on his birthday. One time, I brought him a puppy, but he killed him a few days later." Bitterness burned in his throat. He could still see the poor animal butchered like a chicken behind the house. He had blamed himself for months afterward.

Warmth spread on his hand, and he looked down to see Eala's covering his. "You're not responsible for your brother's crimes," she whispered the usual mantra for his ears only. "Stop blaming yourself for it."

Cathal nodded. His stay on the island had made him slowly realize that. Yes, he had promised his mom to protect Odhran against any harm, and he had accomplished that. Now, it was out of his hands. Odhran was about to turn eighteen and become an adult.

"Has your grandmother ever said anything about her background?" Eala asked, her tone too casual to be anything but. He raised his eyes to hers. "I mean, she must have had a family somewhere, right?"

The truth was he didn't know much about his

Mhamó. Now that he thought about it, he couldn't recall a single time when he had asked about her past, about her family, which was strange since he had always been a curious child. Even the memory of his brother's birth was fuzzy. He remembered his mother and grandmother coming home one day with a baby, but he couldn't recall a pregnancy or any man who might have been wooing his mother.

"I don't think she ever said anything about her past," he admitted, deep creases in his forehead. "All I remember is my mom saying both Odhran and I were the sons of noblemen. When she was not well, she'd rave about our future; that one day, our ancestry would take us from the abject poverty we lived in and throw us into the limelight." He chuckled softly. "She got progressively more delusional after my brother was born. She used to carry Odhran around as if he was some kind of treasure." His eyes got lost in the memories. "At first, I thought it was normal for a mother to act like that, but it was more than motherly love. It was almost as if she thought my brother would be our ticket out of misery. Little did she know he made our lives much worse."

"Maybe your mother was not as mad as you all thought," Eala said. Padraig scooted closer beside them, munching on the snacks his queen had brought with her. Cathal raised his brows. "What I mean is, your grandmother is not who she seems. Maybe there was something to what your mom told you."

He had wondered about his Mhamó and the fact that she looked younger and sprier than ever. Her skin was smoother and her back straighter. And she could hear perfectly, no signs of deafness at all. Cathal had assumed the island held some kind of healing magic.

"Mrs. Ó Broin has magic." Padraig's statement took both Eala and Cathal by surprise. Eala shook her head almost imperceptibly, and the young man bit his lip. "I mean, not that I know that for a fact or anything." Cathal couldn't stop noticing the furtive glances Padraig threw at Eala.

Cathal gaped at Eala, who uncharacteristically hid her eyes under his scrutiny. "What do you mean she has magic? We're common people with no magic traits whatsoever." He furrowed his brow. "Right, Eala?"

"Don't mind Padraig," she said, a metal-melting glare in the young man's direction. "He has a very vivid imagination. Why don't you try one of those sweet buns? Laoise made them especially delicious today."

He was no fool. It was clear she was trying to divert him from the conversation, but why? Was there truth in what the young man said? And if so, why didn't he know? He had lived his whole life with Mhamó. If she had any magic at all, he would have been the first to notice. How many times had they gone hungry or cold? If Mhamó had magic, wouldn't she have conjured up some food and wood for the fire? No, it couldn't be true. Not only were most magical creatures extinct, but magic was not an easy thing to hide.

Choosing to ignore the vexing question, Cathal picked a bun from the small container and stuffed it in his mouth. He would ask his grandmother about it later.

LATER became almost a week. At the mention of Yule, the whole community of swans was set in frantic preparation mode. Cathal had never seen such a frenzy, not even during holidays in Nem. People climbed on roofs to drape bright red festoons from the eaves, clambered up trees to hang shiny baubles from the branches, and dashed from one dwelling to another, placing large flower arrangements and evergreen garlands on doorways, stretching out long strands of white lights from every nook and cranny. The whole settlement was drenched in a festive downpour.

"This reminds me of the old days." Cathal wondered what exactly his grandmother was musing about. The so-called old days were nothing like this. Yes, they had a few happy years before Mother got sick when, even in poverty, Yule had been the one holiday when they all felt joyful, but nothing could compare to this. The old woman sighed and went back to munching on a pastry Cathal had brought from the kitchen. "Are you going to see your brother any time soon?"

Cathal flinched at the mention of Odhran, and guilt immediately flooded him. He hadn't even thought of his brother, much less made any plans to see him. Odhran had the gift to make him feel bad for things that were not his fault, so he had quit visiting him. He shook his head, swallowing the knot that had formed in his throat.

"I'm going to see him today," she said casually, and it lit up all kinds of alarms in his mind. "There is something I need to share with him."

Cathal did look up at her then. What could she possibly have to share with his brother? Mhamó looked nothing but innocent, taking dainty bites off the pastry and brushing crumbs from her shirt. "What would that be?" he asked.

"Something that will make him very happy," she said, a veiled chuckle behind her words.

"What? Mhamó, how can you even want to make him happy after what he did?" For the first time in a long while, Cathal's insides burned with anger. What was with both his Mhamó and mother that made them always wish to keep Odhran happy? "Eala almost died ten years ago because of his cruelty. How can you do anything nice for him?"

The old woman turned her face to him, an odd twinkle in her eyes. "Not everything is what it seems, *garmhac*." He grunted. Lately, it seemed as if everyone in his life had taken a liking for cryptic words. Even

Eala was doing it, and Padraig… well, the young man had become shifty ever since that strange comment about Mhamó. "You'll figure it out soon enough."

He didn't have time to dwell on his grandmother's words. Lily Pad came to fetch him with the excuse they needed his help hanging some lights in the settlement courtyard, the beautifully tended garden which all the buildings in the royal compound encased. Cathal didn't argue. His head hurt thinking about Mhamó's words.

Eala was waiting for him, a sunny smile on her face. He stopped at a distance to admire the beautiful queen he loved so much. Her copper curls fell on her freckled ivory shoulders, left bare to be kissed by the sun. She waved, and her translucent shawl dropped lower. "Come help me, *mo a mhuirnín*." My beloved.

Eala's use of the endearment made his heart quicken and his palms sweat. Her smile called on him like a lighthouse to a vessel. He didn't hesitate, devouring the space between them in long strides and swaddling her thin body with his arms. "*Mo leannán*," he whispered into her hair. My sweetheart. Realizing what he was doing and that there were several pairs of curious eyes watching them, he dropped his arms and chuckled embarrassedly. "Sorry, I forgot myself."

The queen slid a hand from his shoulder and grasped his hand in hers. "Never be sorry for love," she murmured with a grin. She pulled on his hand. "Come help me. I'm not tall enough even with the ladder."

Inside her room, Cathal draped the evergreen

garland and the twinkling lights over her bed, weaving it around the wooden frame from where the privacy curtains hung. She stood beside him, handing him the ribbons to tie it down and caressing him with her glance. Desire made his gut hurt and his hands tremble. He shook his head, trying to control his feelings, knowing all too well he had to stay away from Eala. They couldn't risk enraging the king.

Eala closed a hand under his elbow, supporting him as he stepped down from the ladder. She didn't let go once he was on firm ground. There was something different about her, a brightness that had not been there before. It was as if hope had ignited inside her, and not even the knowledge that in less than a month she'd have to sacrifice herself for her people again could dampen it.

"Mhamó went to see Odhran," he blurted out for the sake of saying something and pushing down the need to kiss her.

"I know," she said. Surprising him into paralysis, Eala rose on her tiptoes and planted a kiss on his cheek. Heat radiated from the spot where her lips touched to the rest of his body. "We're letting him go on his birthday."

Whatever warmth had run through him a second ago was suddenly replaced by ice. "What? You're letting my brother go?" She nodded with such a gleeful expression, he wondered whether she was running a fever. "Why? He's going to go straight to the king and tattle on you and me." Odhran had told Cathal that himself a few times during his visits.

Much to his dismay and confusion, Eala chuckled. "We're counting on that." She looped her arm through his and pulled him toward the door. "In fact, we will make it a point and take him to the palace."

Cathal stopped her. He couldn't understand what was going on. Did Odhran have Eala under some kind of spell? What was about his brother that everyone he knew ended up doing his bidding? "Eala, is everything okay? You seem—"

He wanted to say weird, but she spared him the trouble. "Odd? Yes, I suppose it would seem like that to you. Don't worry, *a mhuirnín*, I'm perfectly sane." He wasn't so sure. "Your grandmother and I have a plan."

A plan? What was she talking about? "Mhamó? She's old and poor. What can she possibly do to help?"

For the second time that day, Cathal was told, "Not everything is what it seems." He was beginning to believe it.

CHAPTER EIGHTEEN

Revelations

Eala

Something inside her had exploded. She wasn't sure what, but she knew something had changed. It wasn't a negative change, much to the contrary. It was freeing and enchanting to feel like that, as if nothing at all could stand in her way of happiness. At times, she chided herself for being overly optimistic about what Cara Ó Broin had told her. The old raven could very well be tricking her into doing her bidding. Witches had had a bad reputation once upon a time. How could she be sure Cara was not like the old wives' tales painted her? She seemed, however, to truly love her grandson and wanted nothing but compensation for his lifetime of misery, serving his cruel brother. The witch looked genuinely fond of Cathal, and that small fact made Eala believe her.

Eala walked underneath a cover of twinkling white lights and sighed contentedly. It was as if the stars themselves had come down to earth to bless them. It had been too long since the last time she had felt this light at Yule. The Guardians be blessed that she could still feel like that. She scanned the courtyard, searching for the man who was in great part to blame for her giddiness and lightness of spirit. She spotted him serving tea to his grandmother under the gazebo in the center of the courtyard. On this second day of the holiday, he had dressed for the occasion, and Eala wondered who had helped him. Everywhere else, people dressed in red to celebrate Yule, but on the sacred island, they all dressed in blue, the color of the sky, the lakes, and the oceans. The swans all wore robes of colors that ran the full gamut of blues from the almost white cloud blue to the deep dark midnight. For one day every year, Earth joined hands with the skies and the oceans and became one.

"Eala, join us," Cara yelled out. Cathal turned his face to her and smiled. Her insides melted. Had he any idea of how she felt every time he aimed those upturned lips at her? "*Garmhac*, pour her a cup, will you?"

By the time she sat next to the old woman, Cathal had poured hot tea in her cup and slid a pastry onto a small plate. "It's your favorite," he whispered. "Jasmine tea and buttery almond." She did love jasmine tea above all others, and there was nothing like an almond pastry to go along with it. The fact that he had been paying attention to her likes and dislikes filled her with joy.

"What do you think of the decorations, Ms. Ó Broin?" Eala asked. The old woman watched the swans as they fluttered from one spot to another, still hanging garlands and straightening plants.

"It looks beautiful, Eala," Ó Broin said, opening her arms in a grand gesture. "It's been too long since I've seen such gorgeous Yule trappings. Thank you for making this such a special holiday for my grandson and me."

The grandson in question offered Eala a shy smile before hiding his flushed face behind a teacup.

Cara Ó Broin leaned over the table and grabbed the queen's hand. "Everything is on schedule," she whispered, triggering a look of alarm from her grandson. She turned to him and grinned. "A week and a half from today, *garmhac*, I will take your brother to meet his father."

Cathal looked as if he would pass out at any moment. His jaw went slack, and his skin turned a pasty shade of white. "What did you say?"

"You heard me," his grandmother said so jovially, you would think she was announcing the beginning of the festivities. "It's time he meets his father, don't you think?"

A strange, strangled sound escaped Cathal's throat, and Eala had the urge to hug him and comfort him. This could not be easy for him. "You know who his father is? Why didn't you ever tell us?"

Cara guffawed as if she was having the time of her life, and for a moment, Eala wondered whether maybe madness was claiming her like it had her daughter.

"I was sworn to secrecy," she said. Then, leaning closer, she lowered her voice a notch. "This is a good thing, Cathal. We are finally getting rid of that poisonous weed."

Cathal paled further if that was possible, and this time Eala covered his hand with hers. "Are you all right, *a mhuirnín*?" The old woman tilted her head and smiled, glancing at their connected hands. "Drink some tea," Eala suggested.

His deep brown eyes met hers, bewilderment and panic reflected in them. "Did you know about this?" he asked, his Adam's apple bobbing up and down.

"Not until recently," Eala confessed, her heart clenching in fear he would be angry at her. "Your grandmother told me a while back but asked me not to tell you yet."

He stared at her for a few seconds before turning back to face his grandmother. "Who is his father? Is he even my brother?" His usual veneer of calm was quickly cracking. She squeezed his hand.

"You're blood relations," the old woman stated, taking another sip of the tea. Eala was having trouble understanding how she could look and act so calmly. "But no, you are not brothers."

Eala felt the shaking of his hand under hers and wished the older woman wouldn't be so cavalier about this. After all, Cathal had spent his whole life suffering to protect Odhran only to find out they weren't even brothers.

"He's not my mother's son?" he asked in a choked voice.

Ó Broin nodded. "No, he's not." As if finally realizing how her words were affecting him, her eyes warmed, and her voice softened. "I know this is a big shock for you, *garmhac*, but everything will become clear soon enough, and your suffering for the past eighteen years will be vindicated."

Cathal snorted. "I don't want vindication," he said, voice as hard as ice. "I feel cheated, lied to. Betrayed by my own mother and grandmother." His eyes rounded. "Are you even my real grandmother?"

The old raven sighed. "Yes, you are my grandson, and your mother was my only daughter. I hate that both of you had to be put through so much because of that weasel you thought was your sibling." Eala thought she detected grief and anger in the old woman's tone. "But this is bigger than us. All will become clear once Odhran turns eighteen."

"For the last time, Mhamó, who is the man I have been protecting for all these years?" Cathal spat out, the paleness of his skin now replaced by the red of rage. "Tell me the truth. Who is he?"

Cara exchanged a quick look with Eala as if asking for permission, but it wasn't up to her to decide. She shrugged, still holding on to Cathal's hand.

The old woman took a deep breath. "Well, Cathal, that boy we brought up is a very important person."

"Who. Is. He?" It was nothing but a whisper, and yet, it sounded as if Cathal was yelling.

"Odhran is the king's only son."

IF Cathal was pale before, he now looked as if every drop of blood had escaped from his body. Instinctively, Eala scooted closer to him so she could catch him if he fell off the chair. She threw a questioning glare at Cara, who had callously broken the news to him. The woman didn't seem fazed at all as she shrugged and touched her grandson's hand.

"Sorry that I'm just now telling you this," Ó Broin said, a gentleness in her voice that had not been there before. "It's a long story, and I will tell you the whole thing very soon, but I want you to know that as cruel as this whole thing seems to you right now, you are one of thousands who will benefit from it in the end."

Eala knew what she meant, but she could also read the pain in Cathal's gentle eyes. Eighteen years of living in hell were enough to break even the most resilient of humans. It hadn't broken the amazing man she'd fallen in love with, but it had to have left deep scars. It couldn't be no consolation to know there was a noble goal behind it all. Not yet anyway.

When he finally found his voice, it was hoarse and thick with anger or heartache; she couldn't tell which. "I understand that you must have had a good reason to do it—at least, I hope you did," he said. "I might even come to thank you for it, but right now, I feel betrayed by the one person who I thought loved me. Did Mom know? She seemed to love that child so much."

For the first time, the old woman's eyes reflected sadness and maybe even regret. "She knew, but she wasn't well. At first, she cared for Odhran as a way to protect your future. She loved you and wanted you to have all the things that she couldn't have; therefore, she was willing to protect and even love this baby who wasn't hers if that meant securing happiness for you. Eventually, as her sanity thinned out, she couldn't separate truth from fantasy anymore. I think she came to love Odhran almost as much as she loved you."

Cathal covered his eyes with a hand and was silent for a while. Eala stole another glance in the old woman's direction. The old witch looked anything but old. With each passing day, it was as if time had turned back a few years, and Cara looked younger and younger. If she didn't know any better, Eala would think the witch was in her early thirties. Had she put a spell on herself to appear older all these years?

"So what's the plan exactly, Mhamó?" Cathal finally asked, his eyes still obscured behind his palm. "Do we just let him go and hope he heads back to the palace?"

His grandmother took another long sip of tea before answering, "No, I will escort him directly to the king. Rian is expecting his son to be delivered to him after the boy turns eighteen."

Cathal lowered his hand and widened his eyes. "Why at that time? Why keep Odhran hidden all these years?"

A subtle smile stretched across the witch's lips. "There's a curse that goes into effect on his birthday," she explained in a low voice. "The king hoped to avoid the curse by hiding the boy until after his birthday."

"Hoped?"

Cara's eyes had gone distant as if she was lost in thought, that tiny smile still dancing in her lips. "He may have misinterpreted the caster of the spell. He's in for a big surprise."

Eala's eyes met Cathal's, and she nodded. Cara had told her most of the story, if not all the details. She knew what the witch was trying to accomplish, and Eala couldn't deny her excitement. If Cathal's grandmother was right, soon, her swans would be free of the threat that King Rian hung over them for far too long, and she would never have to subject herself to her monthly humiliation ever again. Best of all, she'd be free to love Cathal.

"Today, we must forget it all and celebrate Yule," Cara said suddenly, her arms extended to her side in a T, and her face tilted upward to the star-studded sky. "For the first time in many, many years, everyone has a good reason to celebrate." She lowered her arms and looked at her grandson, who was staring at her, slack-jawed and still as pale as the moon. "*Garmhac*, go with Eala and enjoy this night of giving."

As if on cue, Padraig and Lily Pad appeared by their sides, a sheepish expression on their faces. Eala smiled at their interlaced fingers. Maybe they'd be celebrating a wedding in the near future.

"My Queen, we have prepared a feast for you and Cathal in your chambers," Lily Pad said with a slight bow. "It's our gift to you on this Yule night."

Eala exchanged a glance with Cathal, who looked shocked. She hid a chuckle with the back of her hand and then cleared her throat. "Thank you, Lily Pad and Padraig. That was very thoughtful of you." She turned to Cathal again. "Shall we?" She lifted her hand and offered it to him. He hesitated for a moment before taking it and smiling timidly. "Happy Yule." Eala raised her voice so that all the swans around her could hear. "May the sun, the moon, and all the stars keep you safe and happy forever, my beloved swans."

Everyone stopped what they were doing and dropped to their knees, heads bowed. "We thank you, my Queen," they all uttered in unison. "May you be blessed with the same."

Eala curtsied, squeezed Cathal's hand, and led him out of the courtyard. "Are we really going to your rooms?" he asked as soon as they were out of earshot of the others.

She nodded. "It would be rude not to accept the gift." She knew that considering their situation, it was a bit like playing with fire to put the two of them together alone in a room. But her heart was so full of hope, she felt reckless for once. If things went according to plan, she would never again be touched by the king.

CHAPTER NINETEEN

Reckless

Despite the warmth in Eala's quarters, Cathal was shivering. Nerves had taken hold of him, and he had to hide his hands behind his back so she wouldn't notice the shaking. It had become harder and harder to be around the beautiful swan and not sweep her into his arms. Love for his queen had swelled inside him, and it was hard to breathe every time their bodies were in close proximity. The yearning in his gut burned so hot, he often believed it would consume him whole.

Eala had left him at the small table to go heat up water for tea, which meant his imagination had ample time to run rampant as his eyes roamed the room and found her bed. It was a simple but pretty thing, encased in a wall of translucent white curtains and covered in a silky white comforter and pillows. He couldn't help but imagine himself in it, entwined in her arms and legs, taking flight even if only in his mind. He remembered how it had felt, carrying her in his arms ten years ago, before he knew she was human. Even as a swan, Eala had touched his heart in a way no one had ever done before. Taking care of her in that old *scioból* night after night was the first time in his life he had not been lonely. As exhausted as he had been from lack of sleep and working overtime, he had never been so happy, so fulfilled. He had loved her even then—he knew that now.

"Have you fallen asleep?" Eala had returned from the backroom, kettle in hand. She looked at him with an amused smile and a tilted head.

Cathal snorted as his face was singed with embarrassment. Could she tell what was in his mind? After all she had to go through with the king, the last thing he wanted to do was to make her feel like a sexual object, to be coveted and used. He didn't know what he could do to show her that his yearning for her went far beyond the physical. He was no saint. He had had a few lovers in the past, and yes, with them, it had been a merely physical thing, an itch to be scratched. But with Eala, it wasn't like that. With the Queen of the Swans, it went so much deeper.

Sitting down across from him, Eala pushed the kettle in his direction. "Have some tea. You look flushed." Her words made him blush hotter. He took an impulsive swig of the tea and burned his tongue, splashing the hot liquid on the table and his fingers. Eala was on her feet before he could blink, holding his hand and blowing on it as if to cool down his slightly scorched skin. "Are you okay? Let me go get a lotion, so it doesn't blister."

She dashed to the kitchen area again and came back almost right away, a small vial in her hands. She knelt on the floor beside him and took hold of his hand again, spreading the cooling lotion over the burn while igniting an even bigger fire inside him.

"Eala." It was an exhale rather than a word. Their eyes met. "If you keep touching me, I'll—" He didn't have time to finish. The queen bookended his head with her warm hands and pulled it closer, covering his mouth with hers. "Eala." A supplication and apology. He wanted to be selfish and swallow her whole, make her his, and damn the consequences. It felt like a desecration, uttering the name of the king, but he did anyway, "Rian will destroy you and your swans."

She mumbled over his lips, pulling away a little to make certain he could understand her, "I don't care." The recklessness of her words startled him. It was not like her to abandon herself to her wishes and desires. Her blue-green eyes, as deep as the lake, touched his soul. There was hope in them. "I'm hoping your grandmother's plan will prevent the king from ever threatening my people again."

What could the plan be that both women had put a lot of faith in it? Didn't the fact that Odhran was the royal heir only mean more trouble for them? Cathal knew his brother; he would milk the situation to his full benefit. He would neglect to take into consideration that both Cathal and his grandmother had taken good care of him his whole life and turn the king against them. At the very least, Odhran would never let Eala get away with keeping him captive all this time.

"You don't know my brother." Why did he keep thinking of that cruel young man as his sibling? "He will find a way to destroy us all."

She shook her head and brushed her fingers on his cheek. "He won't have the chance." Her voice was a caress that warmed him inside and out. He wanted to believe her, he wanted to have that same hope burning in his heart, but he couldn't help but doubt it and fear what might happen if whatever Mhamó had planned didn't pan out. "Cathal, you know I'll do anything for my swans, but even I have grown tired of feeling empty like something is missing." Her hand slid down his shoulder and came to rest on his chest. "You are that missing part of me, and I am not willing to let it go. I want to know how it feels to be whole."

Cathal knew he should walk away for her and her swans' own protection, but much like her, he had felt empty his whole life. The only time in his adult life that he felt complete was when he had taken care of her all those years ago. Ever since arriving at the island, his heart had soared higher than ever before. He was happy, but he didn't think it could last. Could it be?

Could it be possible that there was a light at the end of their dark tunnel?

"Don't you love me, Cathal?"

A smile warmed his lips. He stood a good foot over her; thus, he bent down to her level and bathed in the light of her eyes. "I do love you, my Queen." And he kissed her.

IT would be easy to lose himself in Eala's eyes. Even though she looked about Cathal's age, her eyes spoke a different truth: deep, knowing, and holding a sadness that was hard to bear. But at that moment, as she yielded to his embrace, that sadness was replaced by something else, a sparkle of joy, of youth yet to be lived. It made his soul soar to think he might be the reason she felt that way.

"Are you sure about this?" he asked again. She had given him her enthusiastic consent a few times already, but he was still hesitant, scared of hurting her and her people.

Eala's dreamy smile turned into a frown, and she held his chin firmly with one hand so he couldn't avoid her eyes. "Cathal Ó Broin, if you ask me that one more time, I may have to turn you into a frog." Her tone was stern, and it made him chuckle. "Don't you laugh at me. I'm dead serious."

He brushed a red lock from her forehead. "You are not a witch, my love," he said with a low chuckle. "You can't turn me into anything but a fool."

A grin replaced the mock scowl on her face. "Have I turned you into a fool yet?" Eala sounded young and carefree. His smile widened.

"A long time ago, even before I knew you were a beautiful woman," he confessed, placing a butterfly kiss on her lips. "Why else would I go for days without sleeping to take care of and talk to a swan?"

She slapped him playfully on his shoulder. "I didn't make you do that. It was your choice." Her gaze softened, and her body relaxed further under him. He could feel every curve, every soft mountain and valley of her petite body. "I'm glad you did, though; I've loved you ever since."

They both went silent then, drinking in each other's gazes. Eala moved first, hands suddenly flying to the laces of his shirt, pulling until they came undone and the crisscross panels fell open. Her touch on the bare skin of his chest was heaven, medicine for his body and soul. No longer hesitating, he shrugged off the garment and covered her hand over his heart with his own. The stampede going on inside him echoed in his ears and was matched by the havoc rising in his lower body. He brushed his fingers along the collar of her dress and glanced at her, seeking permission.

She unlaced her own robe and pulled it open, exposing her ivory, freckled skin to his hungry eyes. He needed to touch her, taste her, have their bodies meld into one. Cathal tentatively cupped one of her breasts, her warmth radiating from his fingers to the rest of the body. He glanced at her again, and she nodded. Leaning lower, he replaced his hand with his mouth.

His senses exploded, and he couldn't tell whether it was merely the physical contact or her special healing gift that made him come alive. Not that it mattered, all he could think about was how she made him feel and how he wanted her to feel the same.

He lifted his head to look at her for a moment, and he thought he heard her groan. "If anything I do makes you uncomfortable—"

She didn't let him finish it, wrapping her legs around him and pressing him against her. "Nothing you do bothers me," she said, voice thick with desire. "You are not the king. You are the man I love, a kind, loving human who I want to keep beside me forever." She swiped a hand on his cheek and smiled. "Now, make me fly, Cathal, make me fly without my wings."

As the last thread of doubt dissipated, Cathal stripped Eala of the rest of her clothes and then himself. Lying together, both naked and vulnerable, was headier than a bottle of wine. He brushed his fingers over her silky skin from the bottom of her elegant neck down to her navel. He kissed the indentation on Eala's belly while sliding his hand between her thighs, ripping a moan from her. Soon, his lips took his fingers' place, teasing, tasting. She whimpered, arching against his mouth, fingers woven through his hair.

Reluctantly, Cathal straightened and sat, hands on Eala's hips and sweeping her onto his lap. She locked her legs around his waist, her heat against his, and whispered, "Make me yours."

Cathal smiled, covering her perfect breast with his hand. "Make *me* yours," he echoed, swelling beneath her.

The queen untwisted her legs from behind him long enough to lift her hips for a moment and sheath Cathal's arousal within her. Cathal groaned, throwing his head backward as waves of red-hot pleasure ran through him.

Did she feel the same?

Even in the fog of ecstasy, he wanted to make her happy more than anything else. He moved his hips like the waters of an ocean, ebb and flow, crests and dips until her body tensed beneath his touch. For a moment, he panicked. Had he hurt her? Had he done something that sparked her bad memories? A moment later, her whole body relaxed, her head coming to rest on his shoulder, a groan of release against his skin. He allowed himself to let go, to follow her in a free fall from the stars to the earth below.

She might be able to fly, but when she fell, he would always be there to catch her.

CHAPTER TWENTY

Escape

She should be worried, terrified even, but Eala found herself relaxed and happy. The smile on her face hadn't faded yet as she lay on her bed, her head on Cathal's chest, a leg over his, and a hand draped over the hard muscle of his abs. Cathal's breathing was slow and steady now that he had fallen asleep, sated by their lovemaking. She could hear and feel his heartbeat against her ear, a song she would never get tired of.

Questions about the effectiveness of their plan still lurked in her mind, but they had been pushed aside by the joy of being loved. Cathal was more than a lover; he was a part of her. Without him, she did not feel whole. If the plan to thwart the king failed, she'd think of something, anything to protect her swans. If worse came to worst, she would take her own life, hopefully thus eliminating the reason the king held them all captive. At that moment, nothing else mattered except Cathal and her lying in that bed, entwined in an embrace. Unlike the times she'd been with the monarch, Eala was not depleted of her healing energy. Much to the contrary, she felt rejuvenated, recharged as if Cathal had given her life, not taken it. A part of her wondered why. Was it because she willingly gave herself to him? Or was it that their union was blessed by the Guardians?

A movement underneath her alerted her. She raised her head to check on the handsome man wrapped in her body and smiled. Cathal's eyes fluttered open, unfocused until they met hers. A generous smile pulled on the corners of his lips.

"Morning beautiful," he whispered, his voice warm and thick with sleep. A shiver ran through her body, warming her up instead of making her cold. "Did you sleep at all?" He slid his hand on her hip and left it there, the heat from his palm sending waves of pleasure and comfort to the rest of her being.

She nodded, too choked up to talk. Eala had read about it; love, the universal healer. There were thousands of books filled with descriptions of romantic love, but Eala never expected to experience it, to have her heart blossom like a lotus under the warm rays of the sun.

"What are we going to do now?" He did not specify what he was referring to, but she knew it nevertheless:

the one thing that loomed over their heads like a large bird of prey, a vulture hungrily waiting. She didn't want to think about it. Not now, not while her blood still ran soothingly warm in her veins and her skin still tingled from Cathal's touch. She would face reality later, but now she wanted to drink it all in: all the sensations Cathal's hands and lips teased out of her, the pressure in her gut, the flutter in her chest. Eala wanted to drown in his love and never come up for air again.

"Let's not talk about it, my love," she whispered, her lips dancing against the skin of his shoulder. "Today is ours alone." They would live the next week as if it was their last, which it might very well be. She shook her head, dispelling such thoughts and sat up. "Let's go for a swim, shall we?"

It took them a lot longer to get dressed than normal, interrupted often by kisses and laughter, but eventually, they donned their shirts and pants and, hand in hand, ran through the front door. A loud gasp escaped both of them; the world outside was no longer green. Instead, the grass and the trees were covered in a white mantle that muffled the island's normal sounds. No birds were singing, and there was no rustling of the leaves in the breeze. Everything was white and silent, serene and beautiful nevertheless. Here and there, colorful flowers poked from underneath their cold covering, determined to see the sun shining gloriously in the clear skies above.

"The Guardians have blessed us," Eala whispered

in awe. Was she fooling herself to read a blessing in the rare snowfall bestowed upon them that day? She chose hope. The Guardians must be in agreement with their union and their plan to depose the king to send them such a gift the morning after Yule. She fell to her knees and bowed deeply until her head touched the floor. "Thank you, holy Guardians."

Cathal didn't waste any time and followed her lead, his knees hitting the hard floor with a thud. "Thank you, *mo chuid aingeal*." His use of the old name for the Guardians—angels—made her smile. Cara had brought him up with an obvious respect for the old ways, before King Rian's ancestors had destroyed the ancient order for their own selfish purposes.

When their eyes locked, both still on their knees, head bowed, something in her snapped free. She wasn't sure of what it was, only that it was a good thing, a sign of great things to come no matter what. Then it hit her, she wasn't afraid anymore. Come what may, she had Cathal with her.

THE rumbling of voices woke her up. The crescendo of sounds reached her in bed and had all her senses on red alert even before her eyes were open. Eala sat up, her heart's mad thumping echoing in her ears. What was happening? She glanced beside her and was relieved to see Cathal, his face still relaxed by slumber.

"My Queen." Laoise's shrill voice came across the closed door. Something had happened. Something bad if her friend was panicking.

She slid out of bed and slipped her nightclothes over her head. She started for the door but then backtracked to cover Cathal's naked body with the duvet. As soon as she let the sunshine in, she knew something terrible had indeed occurred.

"What's wrong?" Now she could not only hear her heart but feel it too, thrumming in her ears in a deafening cacophony.

Laoise's lips were contorted into a rare frown, an odd mixture of worry and anger in her eyes. "That damned brat has gone missing." Her heart went silent for a moment. Was she talking about Odhran? "I have sent the swans to search the island." Laoise lowered her voice to a whisper, stealing a glance behind her queen. "What if the guards find him first?"

"What's going on?" Cathal sat up, the duvet gathered on his lap, revealing his well-toned chest. He rubbed the sleep from his eyes, and for a second, Eala forgot about the reason they were both awake. Cathal had the same effect on her that she had on others; he was her source of healing and serenity. "Something happened?"

"Your brother has escaped," she told him, ruing

the need to spoil his peace. He immediately made as if to get up, realizing a second later that he was naked under the covers. She turned back to Laoise. "We'll get dressed and join the hunt." Shocked by her own choice of words, Eala stood quiet, holding on to the large door and watching her friend rush away. Why had she used that word? The answer came to her right away, clear as crystal: because Odhran was not a human, not really. He lacked a soul, a conscience, the one thing that made someone human. Odhran was nothing else than an animal like his father, conceived in fear and fed on terror. Eala and her people might share their bodies with swans, but they were all one hundred times more human than the boy who had tried to kill her ten years ago.

"How's that even possible?" Cathal asked her as they got dressed in a hurry. "How could he escape all the magic wards and the guards?"

Eala shook her head, her stomach plummeting at the thought. "One of my swans must have helped him." The realization was sickening, that one of her precious and protected people would have connived with such a monster. Who could it be, and why would any of them, knowing all too well that Odhran was capable of murder, help him run away? "I'll investigate and get to the bottom of this, but for now we need to capture him before he goes to the guards and alerts the king too early." There was still one more week to go before Odhran's birthday, and to make the king aware of his son's presence on the island before then could be disastrous to their plans.

As soon as they were dressed, Eala and Cathal left their quarters in the direction of the main square where the other swans had already gathered, awaiting instructions from their leader. Cara Ó Broin was among them, looking decades younger than she was, in a beautiful midnight sky dress that seemed to shimmer as she moved.

Eala positioned herself in front of the small crowd. "For everyone's sake, Odhran must be captured before alerting the guards." She scanned the faces of the swans she loved, searching for a sign: a pair of shifty eyes, a dipped chin, or arms pinned to chest. There was none. She turned to Laoise. "Are all the swans here?" An alarming thought filled her with anxiety.

Laoise turned to the swans for a moment as a wave of whispering rose to the air. "Two missing," she said at last. "Rowan is in Nem on a medical emergency, but Lyra should be here. Padraig, go to her quarters and wake her up."

A knife twisted in Eala's gut. she knew the boy wouldn't find Lyra in her room. The young woman was one of three who guarded the prison cell. They all worked in shifts since there was no need for too much supervision—the magic wards did most of the guarding—but someone was needed to see that the prisoner was fed and had his other basic needs met each day. As if guessing her thoughts, Cathal stole a worried glance in her direction. She nodded and lowered her eyes. What could the boy possibly have said or done to convince the guard to let him go?

It didn't take Padraig long to come back, a frown twisting his lips. "She's not in her room," he said with a shake of the head. After a moment's hesitation, he added, "What should we do?"

Eala gulped, her eyes still on the ground and all kinds of different thoughts vying for supremacy in her head. Cathal touched her arms gently and whispered, "We don't know that she did it willingly, Eala." Kind man, even now trying to protect her feelings. "My brother is an expert at manipulation. She is most likely in danger right now."

She had considered that; that somehow Odhran had tricked the young guard and taken her hostage. Which could only mean one thing, she realized with a jolt, Cathal's brother was going to make Lyra fly him to Nem, the only way out of the island before the next solstice. How quickly it was all a matter of how willing Lyra was or how determined Odhran was to make her do it against her will.

"We have to catch them quickly," she exclaimed, raising her eyes back to her swans. "He's going to try to fly out."

"Odhran will torture the poor girl to get her to do his bidding." It was Cara who voiced Eala's fears. "The queen is right. We must find them quickly. Lyra is suffering in his hands as we speak."

Eala exchanged a look with her lover and was not surprised to read the same fear in his eyes. "Swans, spread out in pairs," she ordered. "Do not try to do it alone. Odhran is dangerous and cunning." She swiped the air in front of her. "Go! Find Lyra."

And may the Guardians protect her.

CHAPTER TWENTY-ONE

The Search

Cathal

The silent prayer didn't offer him any comfort. Cathal couldn't stop thinking of what would happen if Lyra refused to fly Odhran to Nem or, equally as horrifying, if she did agree. The first wouldn't end well for Lyra, and the latter could mean disaster for all the swans. They had been scouring the island with no success. His cruel brother had either already left or had found a great hiding place, which was baffling considering he was not familiar with the island at all. Had Lyra told him about a secluded, rarely visited site?

"I know where they are," he exclaimed, slapped with clarity at last. "The temple."

His grandmother was the first one turning to him, surprise evident in the rise of her brows and the slackening of her jaw. "How do you know about the temple?"

Cathal felt the jab of guilt and stole a glance at his lover. He didn't need to worry. Eala was smiling. "I told him about it, Cara," she admitted. "The temple is not a secret, just something we don't often talk about." She tilted her head in that bird-like motion that always made Cathal smile inside and out. "You're right, my love. Lyra might have told him about it." Swiveling on her heels, she faced the swans who had tagged along with them in their search. "Call the others. Tell them to head to the temple."

In all his time on the island, Cathal had never seen any of them transform. He watched, wide-eyed and open-mouthed as the two shed their clothes and morphed into their swan form, their faces and necks elongating and gradually being covered in white feathers, their arms and hands widening and fanning into wings, their legs shrinking in length as their feet stretched into webbed feet. As soon as they were fully into their animal shape, their swan song wafted up in the air and echoed through the island. Cathal wondered how it felt to change from a human form to such a different species. Was it painful? It looked as it would be, and yet, the swan people did it frequently, and it was part of who and what they were.

Soon, they had reverted to their human form and quickly covered their naked bodies with the discarded clothes. They all set out to the temple on the other side of the island. Even though the island was small, the farthest side was hard to reach because of wild vegetation. It had been an intentional design to keep the guards and other rare visitors away from the Guardians. Old traditions claimed that the Guardians did indeed live in the temple and that it should be protected from non-magical creatures. This had not always been the case, of course. Ages ago, magical races and common humans had lived harmoniously together, but Rian's ancestors had changed all that.

The sun had begun its descent by the time they arrived at the site. Trampled branches and leaves betrayed the fugitive's passage, but there was nothing to see there, only a wall of ivy and other vines growing over the rock face of the hill. "Where's this temple you speak of?" he asked Eala, who had unsheathed the sword she'd brought with her and was busy scanning the area.

Eala stepped closer to him and touched his arm. "Right in front of us, a few feet ahead," she whispered. "I was here a little while ago, but the vegetation has already covered the entrance. We'll wait for the others to arrive."

They all grew silent, not wanting to give away their presence. Cathal barely moved, afraid that even the slightest of movements would alert his brother. If they had been wondering whether the young woman was being held hostage, the scream of pain that erupted from behind the green wall erased all the doubts. Eala exchanged a glance with Cathal, and he gulped. Odhran was not his real brother, but they had grown up together, and Cathal had done his best to teach him how to be a decent human being. Odhran's cruelty filled him with shame and an overwhelming sense of failure.

"Stop blaming yourself for this, Cathal." It was his grandmother, now at his side. "Odhran has the blood of the king in his veins and the DNA of a murderer. He's the result of decades of cruelty and abuse. Nothing you could teach him would have changed his personality. He was bred to be evil."

Cathal's head snapped toward her. What was she saying? "What do you mean by bred? Can't humans change if taught to be good?"

She stepped even closer, her voice a mere whisper in the breeze, "Not if they were magically engineered."

Cathal opened his mouth, but the question never left his lips, for the others had arrived, some by foot, others flying. He averted his eyes as those morphing back into their human form covered themselves with the clothes his grandmother produced out of thin air. If she had all this magic in her, why hadn't she conjured food when they were hungry or wood for the fire when they were cold? Even now, his Mhamó was a mystery, both familiar and a stranger to him.

Without as much as a word, Laoise stepped forward, and faster than the eye could follow, chopped off all the vines covering the entrance to the cave temple. As soon as the brush was cleared, Cathal saw them: Odhran's fist still lifted and ready to come down on the terrified young woman's face leaning against the altar, his other hand gripping her hair tightly. His brother raised his head to look at the newcomers, and a scowl of both anger and loathing twisted his lips.

"Let her go, Odhran!" Cathal said, his hand raised in pleading. "You're in no danger. We're taking you to meet your father later this month." The words had escaped his mouth before he could stop them. He stole a glance in his grandmother's direction, but she didn't seem upset. He took that as permission. "You're a royal, Odhran. The swans won't harm you. They are taking you to the king as a peace offering." His brother's wild, cruel eyes burned into his. "You're his only son and heir."

Odhran lowered his fist and let go of the girl, who slumped all the way to the stone floor. "You're just trying to trick me."

Cathal sighed. "When was the last time I lied to you? When was the last time I didn't step up and protect you?" Even someone as amoral as his brother could see that…he hoped. "You know what I went through, so you wouldn't have to, right?"

The royal heir's face relaxed. "Why are you telling me this now?"

"Because I didn't know until recently." There was no point in hiding the truth—at least the part of the truth that might convince Odhran to do their bidding. Knowing his brother, he was already making plans for revenge against all the swans. "We will take you to the palace soon. No one will hurt you, I promise."

"If that's true, then why keep me in prison?" He had never been very smart, led by his most basic instincts and unnatural desires, but he wasn't totally devoid of intelligence and cunning.

"Because they can't afford the risk of you killing any more swans," Cathal said. "All you have to do is be patient for a few more days, and we will take you to the king."

He squinted at his brother. "What do you get from this?"

Cathal breathed a sigh of relief; the young swan was still alive even though badly battered. Cathal went for one of the truths. "I get rid of you. No more taking the blame for you. I can go on with my own life without worrying about you." He hadn't asked about the swans, so Cathal volunteered, "As for the swans, they score points with the king by returning his long-lost son to him." The smirk on Odhran's face told him he would never let that slide. Once with the king, Odhran would do his worst. He would make sure the swans paid a high price for his capture. Cathal took comfort in the knowledge his brother wasn't aware of the whole story.

Odhran was quiet for a moment, his beady eyes bouncing from Eala to Cathal and his grandmother, who was unrecognizable in her present shape, younger and more vital than they had ever seen her. Then, he glared at his brother and said, "All right. I will let you all stick me in that jail for a few more days if you swear on your honor you're telling me the truth."

Cathal almost smiled. For once, his stupidly naive sense of honor served him right. Even his brother knew he wouldn't lie. He placed a hand over his heart and said, "I swear on my honor and my mother's soul that I am telling the truth."

Which, of course, he was.

ODHRAN was behind the magical barrier of his cell again. He had walked all the way back surrounded by the swan people, all too willing to make him hurt should he try to escape. Despite his brother's promise, Odhran was obviously smart enough not to ruffle any more feathers, especially now that he knew his true ancestry. Cathal didn't doubt that in his head, Odhran was already making grand plans for both a life of luxury and cruelty against those less powerful. It didn't matter that he knew him not to be his biological brother, Cathal had brought him up, and he couldn't break those brotherly ties as much as he wished he could. Inside him, a storm raged where whirlwinds of guilt vied with gales of relief. Wasn't it wrong to feel relieved that his brother would meet his comeuppance soon?

"What do we do now?" he asked Eala. He braced his elbows on his knees, head slumped forward in utter exhaustion. Nothing had changed when it came to his brother; he still sucked Cathal's life out of him. Even after a night of sleep, Cathal still felt as if he had fought a dragon.

Eala sat in the chair next to his and placed a warm hand on his thigh. "Now, we go swimming." Cathal straightened his back and glanced at her in surprise. "It will rejuvenate us. There is nothing else we can do right now but wait for the end of the year when we can finally deliver him to the king. So, why should we wear ourselves thin with anxiety?" She leaned in and placed her cheek against his shoulder. "We might as well enjoy ourselves, cherish the time we have together." While it lasts. She didn't say it, but he heard it anyway.

Hand in hand, they strolled down to the lake, the sun shining brightly above them, its warmth kissing their skin, a mother comforting her children. As soon as the water was in sight, Eala dropped Cathal's hand and began running toward it, shedding her clothes as she went. "The last one is a slug," she yelled back with a chuckle, throwing one of her shoes at Cathal.

Lightness replaced the darkness inside him, and he couldn't help but laugh. "Oh no, you don't," he yelled back, taking off at a trot. "I'm faster than you, my love."

Eala dove into the water first, her beautiful body

glittering in the sun before submerging in the blue waters. Cathal was right behind her, diving into the warm lake with a splash. They met underwater, cheeks swollen with reserved air and hair floating around their faces. His queen was perfect, every inch of her body a testament to her inner beauty and kindness. As soon as both their heads broke the surface of the water, he swam closer and drew her to him, his arm encircling her waist until her small breasts were crushed against his chest, their bodies naturally melding into each other.

"Whatever happens," he said, his lips hovering over her ear. "I will always be thankful for this time with you. I waited for you my whole life, and I can barely believe you are here finally."

Eala flattened her cheek onto his chest, and he tightened his embrace. "You brought me back the sunshine." Her words caressed him, and a shiver of pleasure ran through him. "Thank you, my love."

By the time they went back to the room, pleasantly spent, the sun was beginning to drop on the horizon. Much to their surprise, they found Cathal's grandmother waiting for them. She sat at the table, every inch of her royal and powerful, with a pot of tea and a platter of pastries.

"Come join me, you two." Even her voice didn't sound like the grandmother he had known his whole life. It was hard to reconcile this much younger woman with the wrinkled, hard-of-hearing, stooped old woman he had always associated with his Mhamó. But beneath the smooth skin, the bright eyes, and the thick raven hair, his old grandma, the only woman besides his mom who cared for him, was still there.

They sat around the table and watched her pour them some tea. "What's going on, Mhamó?" he asked, his chest contracting with anxiety. There were many secrets, many hidden variables to their story, it was hard not to dread the worst every time his grandmother came to see them.

Cara smiled and put the teapot down. "Why do you think something is going on?"

Cathal almost laughed. "Because you're here, and the only time we see you lately is when you have some new secret to reveal." Eala covered his hand on the table and squeezed it.

"I guess that's fair," Cara said. "No secrets today, just visiting." He found it very hard to believe, but he took a sip of the hot tea, the warmth sliding down his throat and soothing his nerves. "But you must have questions." He had many questions; in fact, there were so many, he couldn't even articulate all of them coherently. "Ask me, and I will answer if it's the right time."

Despite knowing the need for all the secrecy, Cathal hated all the cryptic talk and the ominous cloud that always seemed to hang over everything Cara said.

The question erupted before he even knew what he was going to ask. "Who is Odhran's mother?"

Cara glanced at him, a subtle smile stretched on her lips. She didn't answer right away, taking her time to drink some tea and take a bite of one of the pastries. Eala, beside him, squeezed his hand tighter, knowing all too well that question had been festering in his brain for a while now.

"Is it my mother?" His voice shook. Had his mother been one of the king's many concubines? He had heard the stories about how Rian had been searching for a woman who could give him an heir, how he had forced families to give up their unmarried daughters for him to bed. He had also heard the stories about how the king beheaded all of them after he found out they wouldn't bear his fruit. His mother was mentally ill, but she had been alive.

"Yes and no." Another cryptic answer. Anger boiled in his chest. For once, he wished he could get a straight answer from her. "Don't be upset. I'll explain."

"How can she be and not be Odhran's mother?" Eala asked.

The older woman wiped her lips on a napkin. "She nursed and took care of the baby since birth, but Odhan has none of her genes." Eala glanced at him, his own confusion reflected in her eyes. "I'm a witch, remember? A powerful one."

Another thing Cathal had trouble reconciling. This was the same woman who allowed them all to starve when she could have conjured food to feed them all.

"I couldn't blow my cover, Cathal," she explained

as if reading his thoughts. "This plan would only work if we could be totally unnoticed by everyone, including the king."

"Why? If he wanted a child, wouldn't you garner points by letting him know about Odhran? Why hide his existence?" Eala voiced the question in his mind.

"King Rian knows about Odhran." Cathal stopped breathing for a second. "He just doesn't know where he is. He expects his son to be delivered to him shortly after his birthday."

The story was becoming more and more confusing. "Why would he expect that? And how did you end up bringing him up?" Cathal's head hurt.

"I will start from the beginning," Cara said, leaning back on her chair. "Drink some tea and enjoy the story."

Cathal very much doubted he would.

CHAPTER TWENTY-TWO

Stories Told

Eala

"You are all familiar with the stories about King Rian rounding up one young woman after another, bedding them, and then discarding them like mere trash after yielding no pregnancies." Eala sat back, getting ready for the surprises that Cara Ó Broin was undoubtedly about to reveal to them. "You've also heard about Dochrach, the great witch who volunteered to produce a king's heir." Cathal's grandmother paused. "That was not her real name, of course, and she had no intention of satisfying the king in any way. After all, his royal ancestors were the ones who had decimated her people."

Eala stole a glance at Cathal, who was sitting, straight as a rod on the chair next to her. His lips were pulled into a tight straight line, and his hands were closed into fists on his lap. She reached out for his hand, wrapping hers around it. He flashed her a tremulous smile with a nod.

"Dochrach's intentions were very different from those of the monarch. She banked on Rian's cockiness and foggy memory of the distant past to trick him into believing her." Cara's eyes had glazed over as if she had gone somewhere else. "When the day came to fuck the king, Dochrach did what she had been famous for decades before he was even born, she enchanted him into believing they had, in fact, slept together when in fact, the witch spent the night collecting what she could from the king's sperm."

"You mean, Odhran is not really his son?" Could this story get any more complicated? Cathal's words mirrored Eala's confusion.

"No, he is indeed his son. Dochrach then used her own egg, fertilized it with his semen, and manipulated the DNA so that only the bad traits were transmitted to the fetus." Cara's laughter didn't reach her eyes. "Witches are not gods, but the more powerful ones can manipulate genes and nurture living beings outside the womb. Odhran was such a baby, created to be evil because Dochrach knew he was doomed. She didn't want to feel guilty sending the boy into eternal sleep." She then glanced at her grandson, her eyes focusing for the first time since she had started the story. "She didn't expect his wickedness would make someone else's life so miserable. She thought the boy would be horrible but manageable until he turned eighteen. Once she realized her mistake, it was too late. The wicked boy had already hurt someone she loved dearly, and there was nothing she could do except wait patiently until the day when she could finally rid her family and the world of both the boy and his father."

Eala's eyes widened. "Are you saying you are Dochrach?"

Cathal opened his mouth, but no sound came out, gaze fixed on his grandmother.

Cara trained sorrowful eyes on her grandson and nodded. "Yes, I am. And I will spend the rest of my very long life atoning for making my one grandchild suffer. It was for a good cause, but that doesn't make it right." She leaned over the table a little. "I will understand if you never forgive me, Cathal. I could have made all our lives easy with my magic, but instead, I was afraid to alert the king as to Odhran's location, so we had to stay as invisible as we could. Poverty makes people invisible in the eyes of the rich and powerful."

"How did you end up with Odhran, Mhamó?" Cathal had finally found his voice, and Eala offered him a smile of encouragement. She could only imagine how he felt in light of all these shocking revelations. "The story says the witch left the baby with the king."

Cathal's grandmother nodded again with a loud sigh. "I had planned to allow the boy to grow in his father's care. I wanted the king to fall in love with his son, watch him grow into a young man, and then snatch it all away from him, make him feel what all those women's parents felt when he used and then killed them. What my people felt when his ancestors killed their children, their parents, their loves. But it didn't quite work that way."

Even though Cara had confided in Eala about Odhran's real identity, she hadn't shared many details. She understood why now. It had to be difficult for her, considering many things had gone wrong with her plan. How could she have guessed her daughter would love that infant as if he was hers? Or how Odhran would make Cathal's life a living hell?

"As soon as the baby was cursed, Rian began searching for someone who would hide the baby and keep him safe until after his eighteenth birthday." Cara continued, "That's when your mother got him. Fiadh posed as a wet nurse and, with the help of enchantments, was able to convince the king she was the right person to take care of the prince. I needed to know exactly where the boy was when it came the time to return him to his father." Another quieter sigh escaped her lips. "Your mother was already unbalanced, and I think she fell in love with the baby. So much so that for a few years, I feared Odhran would end up being a good human being and make it hard for me to go through with my plan. Turns out, he is every bit like his father: cruel and heartless. No amount of love from your mother and you has managed to chip away the ice in his soul."

Cathal reached across the table and covered his grandmother's hand with his own. "I understand, Mhamó, you did it for the greater good," he said. "I'm happy I was part of it even if it didn't totally go according to the plan. Really, I'm happy to have been instrumental in the demise of a monarch who needs to be stopped."

There were tears in the older woman's eyes when she raised them to her grandson. "Thank you, *garmhac*. I love you and hope you can forgive me." Eala heard what she hadn't said—the apology was not only for what had been done but for something else, something yet to come.

THAT all too familiar rock had settled on Eala's stomach. It didn't matter that the reason for her flight to the palace was very different from the normal. The mere thought of setting foot in that place made all her stomach contents turn to acid. Her brain knew it had to be done for the good of all and her own freedom, but her heart and her body remembered all her other visits and everything that went along with them: the unwanted kisses, unwelcome touches, the rough sexual advances the king seemed to favor. The power he held over Eala turned him on and would often send him into a frenzy of perverted sexual play. Ironically, the one thing about her that stopped him from seriously hurting her was the same thing that led her to his bed: her power to keep him young and healthy.

"Let me go with you," Cathal asked for the third time. "I'm not that strong or skilled with the sword, but I can be a shoulder to lean on at least." He had an uncanny gift to know how she was feeling, almost as if they were connected. She had felt it that first time they met, ten years ago, and whatever that link was, it had gotten stronger the closer they got to each other.

"You must stay behind, *garmhac*," his grandmother said. "Too dangerous. We don't want Rian to know about your existence." Cara didn't explain why, and her tone of voice did not invite any questions. She was wearing a simple white dress, her black hair spilling over her shoulders and cascading down her back. Eala suspected she would change once in the palace. After all, the king knew her as the great Dochrach, and she'd show up at his door as such. A tiny frisson of guilty pleasure ran through Eala as she envisioned the king's terrified expression when she materialized in front of him.

Cathal was not happy. Eala would be flying to the palace as soon as Cara gave her the green light. The great Dochrach would visit the king first on Odhran's birthday to reinforce the monarch's erroneous idea that the boy—and his court—would be safe as long as the witch didn't find him on that exact date. Odhran would be taken to the palace by Eala as a swan, a fact that didn't sit well with her lover.

"He's dangerous. As soon as he deems himself safe from falling to his death, he will attack you," Cathal had said when Cara had shared the plan with both of them. "He has no conscience, no sense of honor. It's too risky."

"He will be enchanted," his grandmother told him, a hand on his bicep. "As good as unconscious. He won't snap out of it until Eala is out of the palace and away from him. She will be perfectly safe."

"Something could go wrong." Cathal was not going to let go that easily it seemed.

"I will be with her as well." That was a surprise for Cathal. His eyebrows arched. "I will be in my old woman's disguise. The king will only see me as Odhran's guardian, not as Dochrach."

"What about Odhran himself? He has seen you here…" As the much younger woman she looked like now. Cathal didn't say those words, but they all understood it.

"He has not recognized me in my true form, and the few times I visited him in his cell, I was in his grandmother's disguise. He won't connect the dots." Eala wanted to rejoice, to be excited about what was to come, but she couldn't stop the dread that collected like a pool of rancid water inside of her. Cara's eyes softened, and she leaned further over the table. "I'm not going to lie; of course, there is danger. Everything that's worth fighting for comes with a risk. Ask yourselves if you want to continue to live this life of fear, of waiting for that time of the month when the queen has to swallow her pride and dignity and allow the king's filthy hands on her."

Cathal let out a guttural sound as his hands closed into fists. Eala rushed to soothe him with a gentle touch; the muscle of his thigh was as hard as a rock under her fingers. "You're right, Cara. It is worth the risk," she said. "We'll make preparations for it."

As she made to stand up, Cathal held her in place, a hand on her arm. "Wait," he said, voice as gruff as is he had been screaming for hours. He turned to his grandmother. "Mhamó, you must promise me one thing." The witch's brow furrowed, but she nodded. "The day the curse goes into effect, you must take me to stand before King Rian and my brother—" He shook his head, a grunt of annoyance escaping his lips. "No, he's not my brother. His heir." There was more anger in that word than Eala had ever heard or felt from him, the gentlest soul she had ever met.

"But why, Cathal? Why?" Eala gasped, her hands flying to her throat.

"Because I want to be there right before they fall into their eternal sleep," Cathal hissed, his gaze focused inward. "I want to witness their fear and helplessness as they feel themselves slip into oblivion." He sighed and blinked. "I want them to see Eala and me together and know what they will never have her again."

Silence fell. It was strange to hear Cathal speak like that, anger spilling out with every word. But she could not fault him for that; he had been a victim of the royals' cruelty all these years as much as she had, and he carried the scars to prove it. He was entitled to that wrath, to the hate, and to the hope for vindication. The world was entitled to rejoice for the demise of such a hateful king.

Cara nodded again. "It will be done, *garmhac*. You and Eala will have a first-row seat to the moment when King Rian and all his minions fall under the sleep curse. You have both earned it."

Eala smiled then because she could have sworn she heard her mentor, Queen Aoibhe herself, cheer in approval from wherever her soul had gone after her passing. The future looked bright.

CHAPTER TWENTY-THREE

Interlude

On the morning of the last day in December, Cara disappeared from the island and materialized as Dochrach inside the king's bedchamber. Neither Cathal nor Eala were there to witness her performance, but they could imagine what it must have looked like. The king, not expecting visitors that early in the morning, would have still been in his nightclothes, another poor concubine unconscious on his bed and breakfast on the table. Cara had left the island dressed in her plain white robes, no shoes on her feet, but they both knew King Rian would have seen someone entirely different: a powerful witch dressed in her star-studded navy-blue dress, its long train swishing behind her as she approached him with a wicked smile on her bright red lips.

"I'm here to see your son as I promised eighteen years ago," Dochrach announced, her posture as regal as that of a queen. "It's time to collect your debt."

The king squirmed uncomfortably on the edge of the bed where he sat, but he managed a mocking grin. "Unfortunately for you, witch, my son has been in hiding and has yet to surface."

Dochrach feigned outrage, her face reddening, and her hands closed into fists. "Where is the prince? Don't play games with me, Rian."

The threat was so clear in her tone that King Rian had the good sense of shivering in apprehension. "I don't know where he is, I swear. He was taken by a wet nurse shortly after you cursed him, and I never saw him again."

Dochrach snapped her hands open alongside her body, and sparks exploded from her fingers. "I am not happy, Rian. First, you go back on the promise you made me after I gave you an heir, and now, you hide your son from his mother." Sparks turned into small bolts of electricity, shooting straight to the stone floor and charring the plush carpet nearby. "I will set this palace on fire and burn everything in it if you don't tell me where he is."

Startled and terrified, the king fell on his knees. "I swear I don't know where he is, Dochrach. I really don't." The witch raised her hands in his direction, setting a small basket on fire by the bed. Rian lowered his head all the way to the floor in abject submission. Dochrach allowed herself a satisfied smile. "I will give you whatever you want. Just ask."

The room fell silent for a moment while Dochrach pretended to think. "You will reinstate the few surviving witches as full citizens of Nem and give me the highest noble title in the land."

Without ever lifting his head, the king grunted his agreement, "Whatever you want, it's yours."

"If you fail me, little King," the witch continued, her voice seeming to grow and echo between those walls. "If you so much as hesitate in keeping to your promise, I will be back and burn your kingdom to ashes."

With a wave of her hand, the witch vanished, leaving only the smell of burned wicker and wool behind her to remind the monarch she meant every word she said.

The stage for his demise had been set.

CHAPTER TWENTY-FOUR

Delivery

Eala

The message had been sent. The king now knew that his precious heir was in the hands of the Swan people, and unless he sent a signed, legally binding document promising the release of all swans, including their queen, the boy would remain in hiding for the rest of his life. They all knew that Rian would not honor such an agreement, but they had to play the game in order to erase any suspicions the monarch might have. Let him think they were naive enough to believe he would let Eala go free once his son was safe in the palace.

The response came only a few short hours later attached to the leg of a carrier pigeon: a small document signed and carrying the royal seal promising Eala and her swans a future unattached from his influence or power. Even though Eala knew it to be worthless, she kept it in a safe place, a solid sign of hope.

"I don't like this," Cathal said yet again, brushing his fingers gently over her cheek. They were lying side by side in bed, their bodies turned to face each other, faces so close, Eala could feel the warmth of his breath on her lips. "The king can't be trusted, and you're flying into a trap. You know that as soon as he has his son by his side, he'll turn on you."

Eala touched her lips to his in a brief kiss. "Yes, we know that, but he won't hurt me. I'm his most precious commodity. I'm what keeps him young and vital. He will not hurt me."

"But he might keep you prisoner instead of allowing you to return to the island," Cathal pressed on, his brows knitted in worry.

"Even if he does, it won't be for long." Eala ran her fingers through his short, thick hair, relishing the mixture of coarse and velvety texture. "Your grandmother will make sure of that."

Cathal lowered his eyes. "I feel useless," he confessed in a whisper. "I feel I should be doing something, anything, to help, but instead, I'm staying safely behind and chewing my fingers to the bone."

Eala chuckled softly, reaching for his hand. "Please, don't," she whispered as she brought his fingers to her lips and kissed them. "I really like your fingers, my love." Cathal's lips stretched into the smile that always bewitched her. "Your time to help will come." Not that she understood what his role in the whole plot was. The witch was tight-lipped about it, dropping vague hints here and there that suggested Cathal had a big role to play besides the one he had already: putting up with and being punished instead of Odhran to keep him hidden from prying eyes. But whatever that was, Cara wasn't talking, and Eala didn't want to further stress her lover.

"I know I'm not skilled in the craft of war like you and your swans, but I'm not weak either." All the training with Laoise had built Cathal's already well-toned muscles and shaped him into a fierce warrior. Eala loved that he was so unaware of his own strength and skills. A lifetime of melding into the background had left Cathal blind to his own merits. She kissed his nose and then his lips, a whirlwind of heat curling low in her body. "I want to protect you, Eala." There was so much yearning in those few words, tears sprung in Eala's eyes. "I want to be your knight in shining armor, to be the wall between you and any danger, and be the one you run to when you need comfort. You're a strong, amazing woman who doesn't need me or anyone to champion for her, but I want to nevertheless. I want to be your hero."

Eala's voice came out hoarse and thick. "You *are* my hero, Cathal. You've opened up my heart and allowed me to feel again. You showed me how powerful love is and gave me hope." She took a long deep breath, nestling her head against his neck. "For more years than I can account for, I lived without hope, shedding my humanity into its barest minimum so I could survive and protect my people at any price. I built a wall around my heart that only allowed loyalty and love for my swans through." She closed her eyes, inhaling his fresh scent. "You changed all that. You broke through those defenses and made the light shine through again. I've never been this happy, not since I was a child, unburdened by the crown and the knowledge of wickedness. Thank you, my love."

Eala would be flying Odhran to the palace the next morning, and Cara would meet her there. What happened after that was everybody's guess. Cathal was right about one thing: she didn't think the king would let her leave the palace this time. Not easily anyway. He would want to make sure she was around when the time for renewal came, a day that was quickly approaching. As for Cara, she was certain the king would throw her in prison and execute her as soon as possible. He wouldn't want any witnesses to the prince's return and the breaking of a royal promise. There was no need to worry about Cara, of course, because with her powers, she could easily save herself, but it still made Eala nervous to know they were willingly putting themselves in harm's way.

"Eala," Cathal called against the top of her head. She grumbled an acknowledgment, unwilling to move from the coziness of his embrace. "Promise me that you'll be careful." She nodded, her chin rubbing against his clavicle. "Promise me that you'll come back to me."

She lifted her head and looked at him, diving deep into his bottomless gaze. "No matter what happens, nothing on earth will prevent me from coming back to you. No winds, no rains, no storms, no kings. I *will* find my way back." It was no idle promise to comfort him. She fully meant it. She'd be back one way or another.

CATHAL'S haunted eyes would follow her for the rest of the day. Eala understood how he felt, that sense of impending doom hovering over them, the gut-wrenching feeling of not knowing what their future held. Early that morning, Odhran had climbed onto her swan body, magically lighter and blissfully unaware of his surroundings, and she had flown him to Nem, anxiety weighing heavy in her heart. As planned, they had landed near the palace to allow Eala to change back to her human form and meet with Cara, who was already fully into her old woman persona.

On foot now, they headed to the palace's main gates, Odhran treading along like a child, deep into the enchantment Cara had weaved in his brain. He wouldn't snap out of it until they were standing in front of the king. Eala was unaccustomed to entering the palace this way, normally flying straight to the balcony in her room, up in the royal wing. She was not sure which way she preferred. One meant a couple nights of pure torture and humiliation, while the other could mean disaster.

Or freedom.

She had to remind herself of that, to stay positive and focus on the reason why they were risking it all. She glanced at Cara, nodded, and stepped through the heavily guarded gates to the palace without as much as a blink from the guards. Whatever spell the witch was using, it allowed them to wander in without a glitch through the bustling inner courtyard, the heavy traffic corridors, and hallways, all the way into the throne room where the king would be holding court at this hour. The three of them passed the long line of people waiting for an audience with the monarch in the antechamber and opened the heavy dark door.

Like all the others outside the throne room, King Rian didn't notice them at first, continuing with his business as a farmer kneeled before him, head all the way to the floor. "You did not pay your stipend this month, which makes you a criminal," the king said, his voice hard and jagged like a weapon. He looked up for a moment. "Guards! Throw this man in the dungeon and send someone to his house to kill his family."

Eala couldn't wait any longer and pleaded with Cara using her eyes to drop the enchantment. She wanted to save the life of this poor man and his family, whose only crime seemed to be being poor. The witch understood her silent plea and removed the spell. Suddenly, everyone in the room except the farmer, who was still curled into a turtle position, crying and begging, looked in their direction. Beside her, Odhran also woke up from his magically induced oblivion, studying his surroundings with interest. Cara had promised she would give him memories of arriving at the palace without any help from magic, and it seemed as if she had.

"Queen Eala?" The monarch, usually collected and sure of himself, seemed a little thrown off by the sudden appearance of the three in his courtroom. "What are you doing here? It's not that time yet, is it?"

Eala bowed slightly, sticking to the pretense of respect and fear. "Your Majesty, no, it's not. As part of our agreement, I am here to deliver your heir to you."

Rian's face morphed from surprise to delight. A smirk she knew well stretched across his lips, the smile of a man who thought he had the upper hand. "Oh yes, how could I have forgotten?" His beady eyes, so much like his son's, trained on the boy. "Is this Ríoga? How can I be sure he is who you say he is?"

Odhran stepped forward to talk, but Eala spoke first, "He answers to the name of Odhran; the name he has known his whole life while being taken care of by Cara Ó Broin." She pointed at the old woman beside them. Playing her part, Cara had her chin tucked in and eyes on the floor. "As you know, your prince was given a crescent-shaped scar before being handed to his wet nurse for safekeeping."

"Check it!" the king ordered his eunuch. The little man shuffled across the room and held out his hand to move Odhran's now long hair out of the way. The boy grunted and slapped the man's hand away. "Don't be foolish, boy. Let my man check your neck."

Reluctantly, Odhran allowed the eunuch to examine the side of his neck where the scar was. "He does indeed have the scar, Your Majesty."

Rian straightened in the wide throne, the gold spikes behind him glistening in the morning light. "If this is truly Ríoga, where is his wet nurse?"

Cara, head still bowed and her back hunched, stepped forward. "Your Majesty, she was my daughter, but she passed away many years ago." Her humble voice belied everything Eala knew about the witch. "I brought up the boy myself."

The king was silent for a moment, studying the young man who claimed to be his son. Odhran had a scowl on his face even then, as if the king himself would never be able to control him. "The Swan Queen kept me prisoner for months," he complained, pointing a finger at Eala.

"For his own protection, Your Majesty," she retorted, not bothering to look at him. "He was determined to kill my swans, and I couldn't guarantee his safety unless he was behind bars. He was treated well despite his attempts at hurting my people and thus breaking the agreement we have, Your Majesty."

After a moment of hesitation, the king let out a bark of a laugh, a hand braced solidly on his knee. "He *is* indeed my son!" He laughed again, the sound reverberating against the high walls and ceiling of the throne room. "Welcome back, my boy. Come and sit next to me."

Odhran's scowl turned into a smug smile as he did as his father told him. The eunuch rushed to place a chair by the throne for the royal heir to sit on. The king leaned over and murmured, just loud enough for Eala to hear, "You are not to hurt the swans, you hear? If you do, you will be severely punished." The boy's smile fell. "They are sacred and are to remain untouched unless I say otherwise. Understood?"

Taken down a notch, Odhran's shoulders slumped, and he nodded, stealing glances at Eala and his grandmother. "I won't touch them, I promise."

The king patted his son's knee and laughed again. "Good boy, Ríoga. That is my only rule. You are my crown prince, and you are free to do what you will. I have dungeons crawling with people you can play with if you wish. Just don't touch the swans."

If she had her doubts about their blood ties, Eala now could clearly see the resemblance. There was no doubt Odhran was the king's only child.

CHAPTER TWENTY-FIVE

Unexpected

Cathal

Cathal was surprised the tile floor was still intact even after all his pacing. Hours seemed to trickle like molasses from a narrow-necked bottle. Where were they? Why hadn't Eala and his grandmother returned yet? What if the king, secure in the knowledge he now had an heir, no longer cared about the benefits of having a magic swan at his beck and call? He would have swiftly executed Cathal's lover like he had done with many other women in the past. Surely Mhamó wouldn't allow that to happen. She was a powerful witch, and Cathal was sure she would do something— anything—to stop that from happening. Wouldn't she?

"Eala wouldn't want you to worry yourself sick, Cathal," Laoise said, placing a tray of food on the table. "Eat something. Our queen will kill me if you fall ill."

Cathal didn't spare the food a second look. "I can't eat. Not until they are back safe and sound." He sat on the stool only to immediately stand again and resume his pacing. "Are you sure we didn't get any messages?"

Laoise shook her head. "I'm sure. There have been no new arrivals of pigeons, and Padraig hasn't returned yet." Padraig had been sent to spy. He couldn't get in the palace, but he could fly over it and check for any unusual movement. "That's good news. Padraig would have come back if he thought something was wrong. Besides, it's barely noon yet. They haven't been gone that long."

It felt like an eternity. Wringing his hands, he corkscrewed around a corner and walked the other way. "What if—"

Laoise stopped him, lifting a hand in front of her. "Stop! There's no point in torturing yourself. The old witch is with her. She'll be fine."

"The old witch, as you call her, is my grandmother, and she was not too efficient at keeping us out of trouble growing up," he protested, needing to be angry at someone. "We were always half-starved and half-frozen, and she never used her magic to help."

He wasn't looking at her, but he could have sworn he felt her eyes roll. "She was protecting you. If she used her magic at all, she could attract the attention of the king. Better if he really didn't know where his rotten child was and thought of him as being so well hidden, the witch could never find him."

Cathal knew that, but it still bothered him. They had gone without food for days sometimes and didn't always have wood for the fire during the winter. He had been thrown in the dungeons and beaten to a pulp to protect his rotten brother because of his promise to his mother. During all that time, Mhamó could have waved her hand and made it all go away. It was not easy to let go.

"Why don't you go for a swim?" Laoise suggested, pouring herself a cup of tea and sitting at the table. "It will help you relax."

"No." The passion in his voice surprised him. "Let's spar. I need to hit something."

A raised eyebrow was the only hint Laoise gave of her surprise. She finished drinking her tea, stood up, and left, closely followed by Cathal. They headed to the training grounds, a wide circular slab of smooth rock, just up the hill from their community. All the weapons were kept in racks inside a small hut. Cathal could only use a few of them: a couple of different swords and this strange whip-like weapon that he had mastered quicker than anything else. He picked a heavy sword instead. He wanted to feel each stroke echo through his muscles and bones, the burning strain on his wrist. Anything was better than wondering what had happened, worrying about his lover.

They sparred for almost an hour, sweat dripping from Cathal's brow and blurring his vision. He wiped it with his sleeve and stubbornly raised his aching arm, pointing the sword at his opponent again. Laoise might as well have been strolling by the lake; she had not a drop of perspiration or sign of breathlessness. Somehow that made him even angrier, and he lunged forward with a grunt. The warrior swan easily dodged his attack, swiveling on the balls of her feet and hitting his hip with the flat of her sword. His hip bone protested, hot pain radiating up his side and back. He smiled. Just what he wanted: pain, and lots of it, a distraction as good as any other.

He lunged again, but Laoise propelled herself up onto a large rock. "Stop. That's enough, Cathal," she yelled. "You are going to end up hurt again. How am I going to explain to the queen that it was me who did it?"

Cathal buried the tip of the sword on the dirt in front of him and braced himself on it, the other hand on the aching hip. "She's not here," he said. *She may never return.* His stomach churned. "She'll never know."

"I will have Laoise's head on a pole if she hurts my lover." The familiar voice made Cathal whirl around so fast, he almost lost his balance. Eala was standing at the top of the path, looking beautiful as always, her hair falling to her shoulders in waves of fire. She had changed into her plain white robes, the edges of her thin coat resembling her swan's wings.

Cathal ran, ignoring the pain in his muscles, and threw himself into her arms, a hand cupping the back of her head and pulling it against the flat of his shoulder.

"You're here, my love," he whispered, more of a prayer than a statement. "I was so scared you wouldn't come back."

Eala pushed away to look him in the eye. "I wouldn't leave you in the hands of this swan," she said, throwing a glance at Laoise, who was smiling from ear to ear. "She'd have you in a wheelchair again in no time."

Cathal smiled then, brushing his knuckles on her cheek and drinking her in, the sight and the sunny scent of her. "I'm happy you're back safe and sound," he said, tucking a loose lock of her hair behind her ear. "I love you."

Their lips met in a kiss, relief mixed with desire exploding inside Cathal. He heard Laoise mumble something, but he was too busy relishing Eala's taste to care. Other questions would come later, but for now, there was only Eala and he lost in that embrace.

CATHAL cared less for finding out what had transpired at their meeting with the king than making sure it was really Eala in his arms, keeping her safe against him in the cocoon of their chambers. But the story begged to be told, and soon, his beautiful queen had filled him in all the details about the encounter.

"Odhran—I guess his real name is Ríoga—was beside himself, as you might imagine," Eala told him with a sarcastic quirk of the lip. "To have the king acknowledge him as his crown prince was, I'm sure, a dream come true for him. His first 'royal' act was to try to get his father to throw me in prison." Cathal stiffened, but Eala chuckled softly against his neck. "Don't worry. As I knew he would, the king is not willing to ruffle my feathers too much. He still wants to live and be young for a long time, and he can't do that without me."

Cathal brushed a hand over Eala's wavy hair, happy to feel her head tucked in the crook of his shoulder. He looked up at the transparent coverings of Eala's bed and sighed. "What about Mhamó? Where is she?"

"Odhran has no memory of her as Cara. He totally ignored the woman who brought him up," Eala said, playing with the edges of his crossover tunic. "She said she had a few more things to take care of, but she'd be back as soon as she could."

Turning his head slightly, his lips touching the queen's fiery hair, Cathal squinted. "What else could she have to take care of?"

Eala's body had gone softer in his arms. She was tired, he knew, exhausted both physically and mentally. It could not have been easy to carry his brother—no, he was not his brother—down to the palace while ravaged by anxiety for herself and her people.

"I'm guessing it might have something to do about the curse," Eala said, her voice becoming more distant. "I don't know what witches must do to get their old hexes to work, but she said it shouldn't take long. You know her, cryptic and only revealing what she deems necessary." He acknowledged the truth in her words. "Whatever it is that she has to take care of, I'm sure we'll find out sooner or later."

Her breathing slowed down, and every muscle in her body seemed to relax against him. She was drifting off to sleep. He quieted down, allowing her the silence she needed to fully fall asleep and rest. He was perfectly content laying in her bed, holding her while she slept.

Cathal must have fallen asleep because the next thing he knew was that the sunshine outside had been replaced by the dark cloak of the night. Eala was still fast asleep beside him, one arm draped over his chest, her red hair spilled on the white pillow, a fiery halo framing her porcelain face. Careful not to wake her up, Cathal shimmied his way from under her hold, placed a light kiss on her forehead, and slid off the bed. After covering her with a duvet, Cathal stretched quietly, slipped his feet into his shoes, and went outside, making sure to close the door behind him.

The cool air of the late evening filled his lungs, and, for a moment, he stood there, not stirring, staring up at the velvet sky and the brilliant stars that studded it. He had many questions and just as many doubts about how this whole curse thing would pan out for them. He had been so worried about what might happen to Eala that he hadn't had time to consider all the implications. For instance, once the whole court was asleep, who would rule the kingdom? The king had no other relatives that he knew of. There had been a brother many years ago, Cathal remembered Mhamó and his mother telling him about. He was rumored to have been very different from Rian, decent and kind, but he had died before Cathal was born and had left no heirs. Mhamó had always claimed he had been murdered by his own royal brother to make sure there were no other contenders for the throne. So, who could possibly take the crown? Was there someone in his grandmother's mind? Someone she had kept secret like everything else, and would this person be a better ruler than King Rian ever was?

Two arms slid around his waist and knotted over his chest from behind. He smiled. "What can my sweet lover be thinking of this beautiful night?" Eala whispered.

"Thinking of you, my Queen," he said, covering her hands with his. He turned around to face her. "Thinking about how much I love you."

Eala smiled. "Liar. You were so far away, you didn't even hear me come."

He chuckled. "That's because you are as light as a fairy. You probably flew, didn't you?"

"Am I interrupting something?" The familiar voice startled them, and they turned around toward Cara.

She was back in her true form, a woman in her early thirties, beautiful and vibrant. "Can we talk?"

Cathal slipped his hand in Eala's and interlaced their fingers. They followed the witch back inside and sat around the table and a pot of tea Cara had magically brewed. "Where were you?" Cathal asked, pouring tea for all three of them. "Are you done with whatever it was you were doing?"

Cara laughed. "Is this your not-so-subtle way of asking me what I am up to?"

"Did it have anything to do with the king?" Eala asked, taking a sip of the hot aromatic tea. "When will the curse be activated?"

The witch's smile died on her lips. "By the end of tomorrow, there won't be anyone awake in court with a few exceptions. A few good people managed to somehow survive his reign of terror, and I won't punish them for what they are not guilty of," she said, her lips barely moving.

"Mhamó, once everyone is in a coma, who will rule the land?" Cathal asked, putting the teapot down and leaning over the table slightly. "There are no heirs, no rightful contenders to the throne. The kingdom will fall into chaos."

A strange expression dawned on Cara's face. "Do you think, *garmhac*, that I wouldn't have planned for that too?" Her eyes narrowed, trained on Cathal's face. "I had to keep many secrets all these years, some of which you may not like too much."

"What do you mean, Mhamó? What won't I like?"

Eala squeezed his hand and threw him an anxious glance. "Yes, Cara, what exactly do you mean by that?"

"Remember all those times when you asked your mother and me about your dad?" the witch said, a sad smile stretching her lips. "We always told you he was dead."

A sickening feeling settled in his stomach. "Mother told me he was a nobleman," he said quietly, dread filling his lungs.

"Well, neither of us was lying," Cara said, taking a long sip of her tea. She put the cup down and stared at it for a long while as if studying it. Then, she raised her eyes to Cathal again. "He *is* dead. He's been dead since before you were born. And he was a nobleman." She paused. "In fact, he was more than that. He was royalty."

The tea he had drunk threatened to make a comeback. "What are you saying?"

"Your father was King Rian's only brother," the witch said, her voice merely a whisper and intense eyes still trained on her grandson.

"But that would mean that Cathal…" Eala let it hang as if she was afraid of uttering it out loud.

"Yes," Cara sighed. "That means that after tomorrow Cathal is the new King of Nem."

CARA had fought against letting Cathal do it, but in the end, he got his way. For a second time in less than twenty-four hours, Eala carried a full-size adult male between her powerful wings all the way to Nem. The witch met them by the palace and performed her magic that once again allowed them to walk in without being noticed by the guards.

"This is foolish, you know," Cara said for the tenth time. "What difference does it make whether you talk to him before he slips into a coma?"

Cathal clenched his teeth. Of course, it would make all the difference. He had promised himself he would rub it in the king's face, and nothing would stop him from having this tiny slice of vindication. He was going to tell the king what was about to happen and who he really was. His identity as the new king was not something that felt right or that he looked forward to. In fact, he had been in a state of denial since his grandmother had revealed it to them. It was as if the news of his impending royalty was still floating on the surface of his consciousness, not quite sinking in yet.

The King of Nem was sitting on his large throne with Odhran beside him. No one else was in the room, not even the ever-present eunuch. For a moment, the shock of seeing the three of them back in the palace froze them, but soon, the royal heir flew off his seat, striding toward Cathal and Eala, his finger pointed at them.

"You have a nerve showing up here," he yelled

out, spittle flying from his lips. "I promised Father I wouldn't touch the swans, but I never promised not to hurt you, my *brother*." The last words were spat out with hate. It didn't surprise Cathal.

Cara raised her hand between them, and Odhran hit an invisible wall. He growled like a rabid dog.

"You shall not do such thing, my grandson," the witch said. Cathal was rewarded with a grimace of surprise from his brother. "Yes, I am your sweet Mhamó, Odhran. The same one that brought you up and delivered you to your father."

The king sprung to his feet. "What do you mean? His grandmother is an old woman."

Cara cackled for effect, and Cathal almost laughed. "Appearances can be deceiving, little King. You've been played."

Silence dropped and muffled everything for a moment while the king and his son digested the news. Confusion clouded their eyes, and Cathal felt something inside him relax as if that stone of resentment he hadn't been aware he was carrying all these years was finally dissolving into dust.

Cathal stepped forward, his hand around Eala's. "Yes, King Rian, you've been tricked," he started. "The curse that you believed you had prevented by hiding Odhran until after his eighteenth birthday is still alive and thriving." Panic tightened the monarch's lips. "In a few hours, you, your precious cruel son, and all of your corrupt court will fall into a forever slumber from which there will be no return."

Rian tried to protest, but Cara must have weaved her magic again because he couldn't do anything but sputter incoherent sounds.

"Of course, you deserve much worse than a peaceful sleep after taking advantage of so many people." Cathal looked at his lover, who offered him an encouraging smile. "You took advantage of my sweet Eala. But no more. Your reign of terror is over, and a new king will rise."

There was a question in the king's eyes as he opened and closed his mouth, unable to speak.

"To answer your question, I am your royal heir," Cathal said. For this moment alone, it was worth being the future king, as much as he abhorred the idea. "I am your brother's only son and the only one left—once you fall into sleep—who can take the crown. You will be happy to hear that Eala, whom you blackmailed all these years, will be queen of her people again, free to do what she wishes, free to fly wherever she wants. Free from you."

Cathal turned to Odhran, who was also unable to say anything. "And you, I hope you enjoyed your few hours of royalty because that's all you're getting."

He watched the royal duo glare at them and at each other, their hands around their throats as they desperately tried to speak.

"Let's go," he finally said, satisfied but sick of looking at them. "Cara, give them back their voices."

As they walked out of the palace, Cathal could hear Odhran shrieking like a banshee and the king barking out orders to the guards who were paralyzed by Cara's magic.

Fate was a cruel mistress, and not even the powerful could escape her.

CHAPTER TWENTY-SIX

The New King

Eala

Padraig and Lily Pad had busted through the doors early that morning to find their queen and her man still wrapped in each other's arms, cheeks moist with tears and dazed disbelief in their eyes. The two swans had returned from Nem with the news they all knew was coming but still shocked them nevertheless: the king and his court had all inexplicably fallen into a deep sleep, and their bodies now littered the palace and its grounds. A few other members of the inner court who lived or had traveled outside the palace walls had also fallen asleep where they stood, no matter how close or how far. Cara's curse had been activated despite the king's foolish belief it could be avoided by hiding his heir until he came of age.

"You wouldn't believe it, my Queen," Lily Pad

said, helping Eala put on a fresh robe while Padraig did the same with Cathal.

Eala was numb, unable to react in any way to the expected and welcomed news of their people's freedom. The bomb Cara had dropped on them the day before was still shattering her, deafening her to any other revelations. She pushed her arms through the sleeves of the white crisscross tunic and lifted them so the younger woman could tie it around her waist.

"There were sleeping people everywhere," the female swan continued, unfazed by the lack of reaction from her queen. "Slumped over tables, curled on the stone floors, even half-hanging from chairs and banisters. It was eerie." She shook her head, her usual smiling face a mask of concern instead. "No matter that those people were corrupt and cruel, it still bothered me seeing them like that, you know." Eala smiled at that, glad to hear that the young swan had such a kind heart.

"I checked the king and Odhran," Padraig added, helping Cathal with his boots. He looked at Eala as if asking for permission to speak. She gave him a subtle nod, and he continued, "They were in bed together wrapped in a pile of naked bodies." He hesitated and then lowered his eyes. "There were a couple women with them too, but they woke up when I walked in and ran out in a panic as they realized where they were. I'm guessing they were another couple of the king's female victims."

Eala spoke then for the first time. "It won't fix what was done to them, but it will free them to not fear anymore." Much like herself. For the first time since the startling revelation of the previous day, Eala felt as if the weight she had carried for years had finally faded into nothing. Her people were now free. *She* was free. No more visits to the king's bed, and no more staying up at night afraid of what might happen in the future. King Rian was as good as dead and no longer in a position to demand anything from her.

A smile stretched her lips, and she turned to lock eyes with her lover, the new king. "Lily Pad, tell Laoise that we will all meet in the inner courtyard today after lunch," she told the young woman, who now combed her hair with a soft brush. "And bring the royal guards with you. They need to hear this too."

Both Lily Pad and Padraig froze, their faces blanching. "The guards?" The royal guards had never been allowed within their side of the island. It was not surprising they were shocked. "Why?"

"Some of them might be in a coma too," Eala explained. "Cara made it so only the wicked fell under the curse, but as for the others who are only doing what they must to survive, they deserve to know what's happening and why. Don't you think? They're only human, and some probably have families they'd like to reunite with."

Cathal smiled at her from the other side of the room, a soothing sight for her sore eyes. She couldn't imagine how he felt, finding out he was royalty and that the mammoth responsibility of taking care of a kingdom suddenly fell onto his lap. Cathal was a simple man with humble wishes. All he wanted was to live a quiet life with Eala. After being denied his dignity and happiness his whole life, he was to be denied his freedom again. There was no doubt in her mind that being the king would be like a prison for her lover. He could still renege, refuse to take the crown, but she knew he wouldn't. His acute sense of duty wouldn't allow him. He would accept the crown and be the best king their land had seen in centuries, fair and kind, well in touch with those less fortunate, having been one of them for so long.

Eala would be beside him should he choose to allow her. Now that her people were free, there was no reason they had to live apart from the rest of the population. She could reign alongside him, two kingdoms, two crowns, one heart. She would love and cherish him and make his burden lighter if he let her.

She would be his queen, willingly and heartily.

THERE was a low buzzing that permeated the air and tickled Eala's ears as she entered the inner courtyard side by side with her lover. Cara had joined the crowd earlier, now dressed in muted colors as if trying to blend in with the background. "The focus must be on you two, the new king and their freed queen," she had told them before the assembly. Eala didn't want the attention, and she knew neither did Cathal, who was as happy about his whole new status as if he had been attacked by a swarm of wasps. The only saving grace was that they had each other to lean on.

The droning of voices grew as they made their way to the center of the courtyard filled with her swan people. She raised her head, scanned the small crowd, and smiled, noticing the three guards—the only ones of ten left standing—had joined them as requested. The poor men's faces were painted with a mixture of bewilderment and awe. In all the years they had been assigned to the island, they had never once been allowed in this area or had contact with all of the swans at once.

Eala stopped in the very middle of the courtyard, where a small gazebo stood, and slipped her hand in Cathal's in need of all the strength she could get. He turned his face to her, smiled, and squeezed her hand. Eala raised her other hand, and the humming stopped.

"People of Swan Island," she started with a slight bow of the head that was reciprocated by everyone, even the guards, however belatedly. "I gather you here today to inform you of drastic changes in our lives." She looked at the three guards and added, "And everyone's in Nem."

Laoise, Padraig, and Lily Pad were the only ones besides themselves who knew what had happened and were told to keep it a secret until Eala could address the rest of them. They were not, however, aware of the whole story, and they were certainly ignorant of Cathal's new status.

"Eighteen years ago, one of the last surviving witches placed a curse upon the King of Nem," Eala started, encouraged by the warmth of her man's hand. "You all know the story. What you might not know is that it's true. There is such a witch and curse." The whispering resumed as faces turned to each other, eyes wide with disbelief. She raised her hand again to quiet them down and continued, "My swans are all aware of the prisoner we kept for months now." The three guards straightened and uttered grunts of surprise. "Odhran, whom we thought to be Cathal's brother, tried to kill some of us, as most of you know. It turns out that our prisoner was the Crown Prince of Nem, brought up by the witch who had placed the curse in the first place."

Chatter exploded mixed with sounds of surprise and outrage. The guards instinctively went for their weapons, their faces crumbling as they realized they no longer had them, having relinquished them upon entry in the courtyard. They needed not worry; nobody on the island would hurt them.

Eala allowed them a few moments to express their feelings and then raised her hand again. The voices sputtered to a stop. "The curse has taken full effect by now," she continued, turning to the guards. "Those among the guards who are in a coma were corrupt and therefore just as affected by the hex as most people in court. Those of you who stand among us right now are good people who will be released to your families as soon as possible." The worry in the three men's faces melted away, replaced by hesitant smiles. "The Swan People do not hold you responsible for anything that happened."

One of the guards bowed to her and thanked her, immediately followed by the other two. Cathal smiled at her and gave her hand yet another squeeze.

"The king and his heir are now under an eternal sleep curse with no known cure," Eala raised her voice louder so she could be heard over the whispering that had started again. "Which means the throne is vacant." The talking stopped. Everyone knew that a kingdom without a ruler—even a bad one—was a bomb waiting to explode. "That is until the new king accepts his throne."

Laoise snapped her face in her direction. "But there are no legitimate heirs—or illegitimate for that matter." The king's infertility was well known throughout the land. "Who will take the throne without throwing the kingdom into a war?"

Eala took a deep breath and stole a glance at Cathal. He understood her unspoken words and stepped forward. "I am the new king," he declared, voice so steady, no one would ever guess how anxious he was. "Unbeknownst to me until yesterday, I am the only child of King Rian's deceased brother and the only one in line for the throne." Sound erupted again, a mixture of shock, disbelief, and joy. The swans knew Cathal was a good man and would make a great king. He waited for the talking to wan, then added, "I will be accepting the crown as soon as we can clean up the palace."

It would be a mammoth job as littered with sleeping bodies as it was, but it had to be done. They had discussed it with Cara, and she had suggested a cave on the outskirts of town, large enough to accommodate all of them while protecting them from the elements. Cathal would set up a permanent guard so no animals— or vengeful humans—sneaked inside and killed them. The curse, according to the witch, would last until they died of old age or unrelated disease. Eala knew that without her essence to keep him young, the king would quickly fade into old age, leaving the young man as their only real concern. "But the coma itself will eat at them. Remember, they are not being fed or hydrated, being in a stage similar to hibernation. Even a bear eventually has to eat to survive," Cara had said. "It won't take long for them to fade."

She knew that Cathal struggled with the idea of all those people, no matter how corrupt and cruel, being left to die. It was written in his hollowed gaze and his silence. No matter how justified such punishment was, his kind heart couldn't accept it. Another reason she loved him so much and why he would, however reluctantly, make such a good king for the people of Nem.

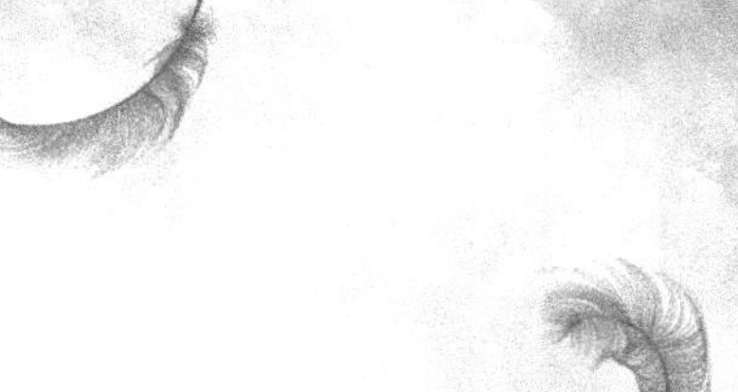

CHAPTER TWENTY-SEVEN
A Swan's Kiss

Cathal

The last few days had been nightmarish as Cathal, all the swans, and quite a few other people from the city went about the grim job of collecting the slumped bodies of those in the magically induced coma and transporting them into the cave that would be their home for the rest of their lives. After much begging, he had convinced his grandmother to alleviate their purgatorial sentence by creating an illusion of life within their sleeping minds. Mhamó told him she had set it up so they would be dreaming of pleasant things, totally unaware of their plight.

Cathal, who had been riddled with guilt, was finally able to sleep at night.

The palace was cleared of the old corrupt court and ready to accept a new one, a kinder, more humane one. Cathal's crowning was scheduled for the first day in February, just a few days ahead. The preparations, both in the palace and in town, had taken a frantic pace punctuated by an underlying excitement you could almost taste; it was in the curve of everyone's lips, the twinkle in people's eyes, the lightness of chatter, and the sound of laughter everywhere. Cathal was the only one with a heavy heart. The moment he took that crown, he would be shackled to overwhelming responsibilities he was not sure he was ready for. However happy he was that the Swan people and Eala were now free to live their lives in peace, he couldn't help but feel the weight of what was to come. He had never wanted that kind of life. Not even in his wildest dreams. All he ever dreamed of was a quiet, comfortable life.

And of Eala.

But could they even have a life together now? Both rulers of their own separate kingdoms, how would their relationship fit in? Would it factor in it at all? Or would they have to make yet again an ultimate sacrifice and let go of each other for the sake of their people?

"Why so glum?" Lily Pad, arms stacked with garlands of evergreens, stood before him, her head tilted in a way that betrayed her swan side. "Aren't you excited?"

Cathal smiled, however sadly. "Don't mind me," he said. "It's all very overwhelming, that's all."

She chirped, her rosebud lips puckered. "Our queen has requested your presence in the main throne room." Her tone was unusually formal, and his stomach clenched. What was going on?

He didn't have time to ask since the young woman scampered away with her load of decorations, leaving him to stare after her. She seemed worry-free, young. Had he ever been that way? He didn't think so. With his brother as his responsibility, he had never been allowed to be truly young.

With his feet turned into lead, Cathal crossed the main hall in the direction of the throne room. Until just a couple days ago, Cathal had never been in the palace, and now, this was his home. He constantly felt the need to pinch himself and make sure he was not stuck in some weird dream.

Eala sat on an elaborate chair next to the throne, her white dress falling in waves of delicate fabric to the floor, and her beautiful hair gathered on top of her head like a crown. Even in that simple dress, she was every bit a queen. His chest tightened.

"Did you want to see me?" he asked, quietly approaching the wooden dais where the throne was set. She turned her beautiful face in his direction, and a smile stretched her pink lips. God, he loved her so much, it hurt sometimes. "You look exquisite, my Queen."

"You're too sweet, my love," she breathed, her smile widening. "Come sit." She nodded toward the throne, and he gulped. He couldn't sit there. Not yet. Maybe never. She tilted her head. "If anyone was ever deserving of that throne, it's you."

He was not sure about that, but he did as she told him and perched on the edge of the over-the-top throne. "My first edict will be to change this horrible ostentatious chair," he said, surer about that than anything else in his life. "It has to go. I want something simple and halfway comfortable."

Eala smiled again. "You should. That throne does not fit you at all, my love, only what it represents." Cathal sighed and nodded, not convinced. "I called you here because I have something to discuss with you." Should he be worried? "You will be crowned King of Nem in a couple days, and your life will change."

His heart fluttered and made him cough. Was she about to tell him they had to go their separate ways? He didn't want to live without her; in fact, he would just as soon be the miserable Cathal he had been all his life than being at peace without her. There was no peace anywhere she wasn't.

"I am also the ruler of my people, and I can't—despite things being easier and peaceful now—neglect my duties toward them." Cathal swallowed the lump that had formed in his throat. "I have a proposal for you, Cathal."

His head snapped up. "Proposal? What kind of proposal?" Despite the fear in his heart, he was curious. Her words were unexpected.

She folded her elegant hands on her lap and licked her lips before replying, "It's as much a political proposal as it is personal." He was more confused than ever. What did she mean? "I ask you to hear me out before making any decisions. Promise?"

This could not be good. His heart was trying to escape from his thorax, and it had become very hard to breathe, but he nodded and managed to utter, "I promise."

Much to his astonishment, Eala stood up, crossed the short distance between their chairs, and stood facing him. The smile was gone, and in its place, there was a mask of solemnity that scared him more than anything else. She closed her hands on the sides of her dress and pulled it up just enough so she wouldn't trip on the fabric as she went down on her knees before him. He tried to get up, but she raised a hand to stop him. What was she doing? She was a queen. She shouldn't be bowing like that to him.

"Cathal Ó Broin, my love and my equal," she recited, the formality of her words belying the warmth of her voice. "Will you consider marrying me and joining our kingdoms into one?"

Cathal almost fell off his perch. Had he heard her correctly? Or was this another one of his crazy dreams of late? "What did you say, Eala?"

She raised her head but stayed on her knees. "I'm humbly asking for your hand in marriage and the fusion of both our people." She smiled then, hesitantly, almost fearfully, she pressed, "What do you say?"

The new king covered his mouth with a hand and

his heart with the other. "You want to marry me? And be queen by my side?"

She nodded, her eyes suspiciously shiny. "I will be the Queen of Nem if you'd be the King of the Swans."

Cathal slid off the edge of the throne and fell on his knees in front of her. "I thought you were going to tell me we couldn't be together anymore," he confessed, biting his lower lip.

"How could I ever do that? I love you. I want to spend the rest of my life with you," she said, shuffling closer to him until their bodies touched. Even on their knees, she was significantly shorter than him, her head barely reaching his shoulder. "Let's rule together. Two heads are better than one after all, right?"

He held her hands between them, his lips refusing to stop smiling. "Yes, my Queen, I will marry and love you forever," he said.

Eala pulled him closer and kissed him briefly. "This kingdom has been ruled by heartless kings for far too long," she whispered over his lips. "Now, it will be ruled with all the kindness and love of our two hearts."

Their lips met again, this time in a longer, better savored kiss. Cathal pulled away long enough to look into her eyes and whisper, "I love you."

Then, he kissed the swan.

CHAPTER TWENTY-EIGHT

Epilogue

It is said that the Queen of Nem was once known as the Swan Queen, and there are those who would swear they often saw her fly over the palace grounds toward the ocean in a flurry of white feathers. But all agreed that no matter how far she flew, the queen always came back to the arms of her beloved, King Cathal of Nem, and their child and heir, Prince Ciaran.

Legend has it that the prince was born on a stormy day when the winds and the rain whipped the land and its inhabitants with merciless cruelty. As soon as the dark-haired newborn opened his mouth for his first wail, the wind died down, and the clouds dissipated to allow the glorious sunshine to come through. The story goes that the room where the child was born lit up with the warm rays of the sun and that the baby's wail soon turned into a coo.

The kingdom flourished under the rule of the royal

couple. They governed with fairness and compassion, their love for their people coming clearly across in everything they did or said. Magical creatures, descendants of those nearly exterminated a few generations back, returned from exile to live openly among the full humans with the blessing of the crown. But the royal couple stayed childless for many years after their wedding, and everyone feared their bloodline would end. When Queen Eala's pregnancy was announced, both the people of Nem and the swans rejoiced about the imminent birth of the crown prince, the much wished-for fruit of the best rulers the land had seen in generations.

On the day of the Naming, everyone was invited to partake of the festivities. Full humans and magical creatures gathered around the palace to enjoy the generosity of their king and queen. A select few were invited inside the palace to share the more intimate part of the rite with the royal couple. Cara, once known as the great witch Dochrach, was there in her capacity as the great-grandmother of the child, Laoise as Ciaran's godmother, and Padraig as the godfather. The other swans spread across the large room, goblets in hand and smiles on their faces.

King Cathal raised the baby in front of him and declared, "This is my royal heir, Crown Prince Ciaran. May he be fair and kindhearted and love his people as much as we do." He turned his face to Eala in a silent request.

Wearing a simple circlet of white feathers, the queen stepped forward to gently touch her son's forehead. "May he never be blinded by greed or fear, and may his smiles obscure his frowns."

The great witch also stepped closer and placed a hand on the baby's belly. Ciaran cooed and wiggled his tiny little fingers in the air. A happier baby had never been seen. She leaned over and smiled at her great-grandson. "May Prince Ciaran always carry the light of hope within and never once doubt our love for him." She closed her eyes for a moment as if listening. There were tears in her eyes when she reopened them, but her smile never faded. "And may the magic in him be strong and never denied."

King Cathal took the baby to the balcony and looked down at the crowd that stretched across the square as far as the eye could see. Silence fell as every head tilted up to watch their king present his heir.

"Help me welcome Prince Ciaran, good people of Nem," he said, arms under the child's armpits, raising him in the air.

The people roared, a happy sound that rippled through the crowd and rose like a hot-air balloon up to the balcony where the king and queen stood.

It was then that Ciaran, the first full-blooded magical prince of Nem, opened his downy white wings and let out a happy chuckle.

The future was bright.

ACKNOWLEDGMENTS

I'VE been in love with fairytales since I was a little kid. Mind you, I was first introduced to the hardcore, scary Grimm's fairytales that had very little to do with the water downed versions our children read today. I liked them all. So it was almost inevitable that I would write a fractured fairytale. In fact, I ended up writing several.

My version uses elements and inspiration from at least a couple of those old stories. One is a very twisted kind of *Sleeping Beauty* (no nice, pretty maiden this time) and the other is Hans Christian Anderson's *The Wild Swans* and Grimm's *The Six Swans* (which are pretty much the same story with slight variations).

I must thank a few people for their support, encouragement, and patience. My wonderful beta readers, Lisa Meyer and Lori Barrett, who always generously offer their time to help me out. Maria Vickers, all around awesome editor and fabulous individual. R.M. Gilmore who formatted this book for me and endured all kinds of silly questions. Audrey Hughey of The Author's Transformation Alliance who encouraged me to publish this book and cheered me along the way. Becky Johnson who believed in my stories and by doing that made me believe in myself as an author. And of course my amazing Rebels & Outcasts who have been so supportive of me and my craziness.

I couldn't forget the amazing artist that designed my cover, Adrijana Cernic from Adriatica Creation. I get lost in her website, lol. The truth is I get often inspired by art and her cover inspired this story, not the other way around. Thank you so much for that.

My usual thanks go to my family who always supports me and my friends who tolerate my creative madness. A special thank you for my paternal grandma, Alice Reis, who was the one who introduced me to all-things fairytales. May you be reading them to the angels, avó.

Readers, I wouldn't be here if it weren't for you. Bookworms do rule the world so I hope you enjoy this fairytale about the magic of love. Keep dreaming.

If you liked **KISS OF THE SWAN**
you might want to check out Natalina Reis's other books.

ROMANTIC COMEDY:
WE WILL ALWAYS HAVE THE CLOSET -
BOOKS2READ.COM/CLOSET
LOVED YOU ALWAYS -
BOOKS2READ.COM/LOVEDYOUALWAYS
BLIND MAGIC -
BOOKS2READ.COM/BLINDMAGIC
HER REAL MAN -
BOOKS2READ.COM/REALMAN/
FICTIONAL-ISH -
BOOKS2READ.COM/FICTIONAL-ISH
DATING THE INTERN -
BOOKS2READ.COM/DATINGTHEINTERN

DYSTOPIAN ROMANCE:
HEART'S PREY -
BOOKS2READ.COM/HEARTS-PREY

To keep up to date with Natalina's news and books,
follow her on the Web:

Facebook:
www.facebook.com/authornatalinareis
Website/Blog:
www.natalinareis.com/
Twitter:
www.twitter.com/TichaB
Goodreads:
www.goodreads.com/author/show/14883335.
Natalina_Reis
BookBub:
www.bookbub.com/profile/natalina-reis
Instagram:
www.instagram.com/reisnatalina/
Reader's Group:
www.facebook.com/groups/215263965917134/
Pinterest:
www.pinterest.com/lisboeta62/

www.ingramcontent.com/pod-product-compliance
Lightning Source LLC
Chambersburg PA
CBHW071420200726
48294CB00002B/465